ICE RINK

By

C. Lewis Colton

© 2018 by C. Lewis Colton, Los Angeles, California

All Rights Reserved. No part of this book may be reproduced in any form by any means without permission from the publisher.

ISBN: 978-1727628388

ICE RINK

Chapter 1
Hockey Action

Home Team 4, Visitors 2, read the scoreboard on the Cedar Grove Ice Rink. The onlookers in the crowd were screaming encouragements to their hometown hockey team. The visiting team's supporters were mostly quiet behind the boards. Laketown defenseman Mike Thomas skated quickly to the left to pickup the ricocheted puck as it caromed off the boards. He moved it deftly to the center with the blade of his stick, spun around and passed left to the team's center, Sven Olavson, who took it across the blue line, then shoveled it into the opposing team's backboards, chasing it in the process. There, it was tied up between him and the Cedar Grove defenseman.

The clock reads 01.35. The game was in the third period. It was only about one and a half minutes before the final buzzer. Laketown coach Josh Steenberg pulls the goalie in favor of another forward, as the team fights fiercely for the puck and a shot for another goal. Defenseman Mike controls the puck after a long pass gone awry by the opponents. He skates the puck across his own blue line, then the red line with a cross over, then to the right across the enemy blue line. From the right side, he fakes a pass to the other defensemen then slaps the puck toward the enemy net with a mighty back swing. The puck is blocked by the goalie, who smothers it, then kicks it over to a nearby teammate. The block brought out a mighty scream of approval from the hometown fans. The puck changes hands between the teams but finally, a shot from a Cedar Grove defenseman from the blue line goes into the empty net for an easy goal. The score, home team 5, Visitors 2. Before the next face-off can be made, the game ending buzzer sounds.

The opposing teams skate by each other doing the usual "Nice Game" five-finger palm slap before filing out of the rink. The coaches shake hands, and then follow their players into the locker room. The Laketown skaters squat down on the benches with heads down. Helmets come off and drop between their feet. They lean their hockey sticks on the bench next to them. Coach Steenberg walks to the end of one of the benches and puts his foot on one. After a moment all the teammates look up at him.

"Listen up you guys," he said, firmly. "We're almost halfway into the season and you guys are still hot dogging it with the puck. You're not passing it around enough. The other team kept passing it around looking for a good shot. They got the shots. We didn't. You guys are just as good at they are. We weren't getting pushed around. Next practice, we're going to work on passing our way down the ice. Got it?"

After a few minutes, the skaters were taking off their skates and pads and putting them into their bags. Some of the parents came into the locker room to check in with their sons. Some quiet talk ensued. Mike's dad walked over and stood in front of him.

"Tough game, Mike," he offered. "I thought we could beat these guys. They looked pretty well organized, though," he added. "Your slap shot looks pretty good. They had a good goalie."

"Yeah," answered Mike. "He blocked everything we threw at him. Our goals were both junk shots that went in."

"Yeah," said his dad. "You gotta have a good goalie."

"Yeah," answered Mike. "That's for sure."

"Mike, another thing, I don't like to keep repeating myself, but you've gotta slow down those guys before you check them. You're banging yourself up. And they're going to come after you."

"I hear you, Dad," responded Mike. "I'll try to remember. Nobody else has warned me about that."

"Well I'm warning you, okay. Just get in their way and slow 'em down before you bump 'em."

Mike finished tying his shoes and stood up. He stuffed his gear into his carry bag and zipped it up. His dad handed him his two sticks and they headed to the exit.

"See you later Smitty," Mike called over to the other defenseman, waving to the rest of the team.

"Later Mike," replied Smitty.

Mike's dad shook hands with the coach as he headed out the door. Mike followed his dad out the rink and onto the rink parking lot. Mike stood 6 foot tall at just about the same height as his dad. They both had dark hair. His dad had a red mustache, but was otherwise clean-shaven. Mike had a profile much like his mother, narrow straight nose with a prominent bridge. When they reached the khaki colored van, his dad clicked open the doors and Mike tossed his bag and sticks onto the back seat. They buckled up their seatbelts and they were on their way home. They were about 18 miles from home. Mike tuned the car radio to a show featuring a clownish host and they listened to the nonsensical material the host bounced his way throughout the show.

"You got any homework to finish?" his dad asked when they arrived at the house a while later.

"Yeah, I got some math to finish. The rest of my work is done. I'm okay with that."

"You going to swim this season?" asked his dad.

"Yeah. I'm the head jammer in the backstroke. Maybe I'll try the breaststroke, too."

"Well, good luck with that. I never get to make it to a meet it seems. I'm always too busy," commented his dad. "Neither does your mom. We both work late hours."

"That's okay, Dad. I had the whole school cheering for me."

"Anyway, Mike, you played a good game. You can't make up for the other guys' mistakes. Things will get better."

They got out of the car and went into the house. Mike brought his hockey gear with him. It was early in February and still getting dark early. Mom was sitting at the kitchen table working on the hand calculator.

"What are you doing, Kathy? Ya working on the books?" asked his dad.

"That's what I'm doing all right," she replied. "Are you okay, Mike? No new injuries, I hope?"

"He's okay, Mother," answered his dad.

"Well I have to ask. It makes me feel better to know things," she retorted.

Mike headed upstairs to his bedroom to change clothes and work on his math homework. The trigonometry was giving him a little trouble. He was concerned about that. He had done well in algebra and geometry, but trig was a little different with its sines and cosines and tangents. And calculus would be something else, he surmised. He took off his hockey pants and tee shirt and put on some shorts and an old sweatshirt. He took a swig from his water bottle and grabbed his trig book with him to his desk. He opened the book to his assignment page and put his hands behind his neck.

Downstairs, Mike's dad, who owned a lumberyard in Laketown, sat down next to his wife. She kept the books for the business.

"How'd we do last month, Sweetheart," asked his dad, whose name was Bill.

"We came out with a small profit," she said. "That's after our salaries," she added.

"Well, business ought to pick up in a month or two, when the weather improves. We have to keep making money with all our expenses, with a daughter at the university, and paying for a kid on the hockey team. He's gonna need new skates pretty soon," said Dad, Bill.

"Amen to that," said his wife.

"Is Angie working at all, I'm mean part time?" asked Dad.

"She tutors other students and they pay her at their study sessions," said his wife.

"Well, that'll help out with her personal expenses," replied Dad.

∽

Back at the Cedar Grove Ice Rink, the Laketown hockey coach stayed around to watch the Laketown Pee Wee team play the locals. He was standing next to one of the parents.

"The Pee Wees have some pretty good skaters," he commented.

"Yeah, they got two solid lines and one of the skater kids has goaltending experience in case we need a backup. They'll do pretty well, I think," replied the parent. "My kid is getting a lot of ice time. We're pretty satisfied with his progress."

"I wish I could say the same for my Midgets. We've only got nine skaters and a goalkeeper that should be out on one of the lines. We got beat 5 to 2 in the game before this one," said the coach.

"My other kid is moving up from the under 16 Midgets next season. Maybe he'll play for you," said the parent. If you're still the coach, that is."

"Good," declared the coach. "I welcome good players. We could use all the help we can get."

A big groan went up from the crowd watching, interrupting the two, after Laketown scored a goal.

"Way to go, guys," yelled the parent next to the coach.

Chapter 2
Public Skating

The Laketown Ice Rink was crowded with the Friday night skaters when Mike pulled up in his dad's pickup truck. He parked several slots away from the other cars to avoid any fender bender accidents that might occur. He held his skates by the strings as he walked up to the entrance. He had on a light jacket over his sweatshirt and a pair of sweat pants. He was wearing a baseball cap to keep his head warm while skating. His long dark hair hung out from beneath the cap. He nodded to the doorman as he walked inside and headed to the cashiers counter to pay his entrance fee. He handed the attendant $3 bucks and found a bench to sit on and laced up his skates. His skates tied, he dug out of the walk around area and onto the ice. He took the skate guards off his blades and put them into his jacket pocket before gliding out and starting to skate around. After a turn around the rink, he spun around and began skating backwards. Since he was a defenseman, he was intent on improving his backward skating abilities. He kept his eye on the many skaters zipping around the rink so as not to collide with one. He bent down at the waist slightly to emulate his style while playing hockey, keeping his eye on traffic over his shoulder.

He looked around once in a while, for any teammates that might be coming to skate. He saw a couple of kids from the younger teams, but none from his own. He took off and changed his skating routine to zig-zagging around some of the other skaters. Mike was intent on becoming expert on the ice.

He was already expert at skating backwards but he knew finesse and expertise were essential to his success in hockey. After a half dozen times around the ice he came to a sharp hockey stop, spraying ice, and stopped to rest against the boards.

He noticed a trio of girls from high school skate out on the ice. They were part of the popular elitists of the campus. One of the girls was probably the best looking girl on the campus. She was so good looking that it was hard not to stare at her. In Mike's eyes, she was the type that you were afraid to talk to. And to top it off she had the body of a super model. Her name was Evelyn something or other. She had dark blond hair on top of a perfectly shaped face. She looked to be about five foot six and carried her shoulders and head well. The girls were wearing figure skates like most of the other skaters at the rink. If Mike were an egotistical guy, he might have tried to wow the girls in the rink with his skating heroics. But he wasn't the type to act stupid and show off.

About an hour after he had come to the rink, he put on his skate guards and went to the snack bar. He bought a bottle of spring water and sat down on a bench. Some kids from the Pee Wee team came over to him and started talking hockey with him. They told Mike what a good coach they had. Mike said he had a good coach too. When the Pee Wee kids left, Mike sat drinking his water and thinking about his obsession with hockey. In the springtime, he would be back on the swim team where you really had to have good form to compete.

Apparently, Mike hadn't gone unnoticed. The three popular girls trudged up with there skates unprotected and stopped in front of him.

"You're on the hockey team aren't you?" asked one of them, a brunette.

"Yeah, I play on the midget team," Mike nodded.

"Why do they call it a midget team? You guys aren't midgets are you?" she inquired. "You're all big guys."

"Well, they have different names for different age groups, the oldest group being the under 18 midgets," replied Mike, shrugging his shoulders. "They start off with Pollywogs, Mites, Squirts, Pee Wees, and on up the ladder. The group below us is called the Bantams. I was a Bantam three years ago," he explained.

"Don't they have a hockey team at the school?" the especially good looking one asked.

"They don't have the money to suit up a team and hire a bus to drive us to other schools," explained Mike, eying the girl nervously. "We've only got club hockey in this town where you have to pay your dues and buy your own equipment."

"Doesn't your dad own the lumber yard on Lakefront Street?" she asked.

"Yeah. How did you know?" answered Mike, keeping his eyes on her face.

"Oh, I've seen you in the truck with him a few times," she replied.

"I never thought anyone noticed when I'm with him," answered Mike.

"You've got a sister in college haven't you?" she went on.

"Yeah, that's right," Mike nodded.

"I saw you on the swim team last year," interjected one of the other girls. It was the one named Laraine.

"That's me too," said Mike.

The three girls sat on the bench in front of him and began talking with one another. Mike sat there, self consciously, not knowing what to do about that. He took a nervous drink out of his bottle and looked out at the skaters on the ice.

All of a sudden the special one asked him, "You want to skate with me?"

"Oh, man," Mike thought to himself. "You mean like holding hands," he asked.

"We can hold hands. That's right. That's what I mean," she said.

Mike thought for a few seconds, looking at her and then said, "Okay, if you're sure."

"I'm sure," she nodded, holding out her hand. "Let's go."

The other girls laughed as the two got up and walked to the rink ice. Mike almost forgot to take off his skate guards.

When they were out on the ice, Mike told her, "The last time I did this was when I was five years old and whizzing around with my ankles turned inward. The older girls wanted to skate with me. I guess they thought I was cute."

His skating partner just smiled at him. Mike was careful not to skate too fast with her being on figure skates and he being on hockey skates. The music being played on the rink was mostly old standards. Her hand felt good in his. After a few minutes, Mike asked her, "You want to skate backwards?"

"I don't know how very well," she said.

"I'll hold on to you and guide you," he said.

Mike took her wrist in his left hand and her elbow in his right hand and led her backwards with the flow of the crowd. She almost fell at first but Mike steadied her and showed her how to move her feet.

"This is the way I skate when I'm playing in a hockey game," he informed her.

After a while he put his right hand in back of her waist. She was getting the rhythm. They skated this way for a while then changed back to skating frontwards. When the music stopped they got off the ice, Mike put on his guards and walked her back to her friends.

"Thanks for the skating lesson," she said, smiling, then turned back to her friends to chat.

Mike sat down and figured he'd take it easy for a while, and then go back home. He would have to help out at the lumberyard the next morning so he thought he had better call it a night. He took off his skates and shook out his stockings. He was still a little unnerved by the turn of events. He obviously hadn't expected to skate with a beauty queen. He put his stockings and shoes back on and got up to leave. He looked over at the girls, saluted them with his right hand at his forehead, and said, "So long, ladies. See you in school." Then he walked to the front entrance to leave. He walked to his dad's pickup truck, got in and sat a few minutes thinking about his night at the rink.

"I don't know if she liked me for my skating or for my good looks," he asked himself. "For my good looks, for sure. Next time I'll have to shave."

He pulled out of his parking space and headed home.

Mike's job at the lumberyard was picking up stray slats and cut boards and putting them into the surplus bin that was set up for shoppers wanting small pieces at discount prices. After that, he took the big push broom and swept up sawdust deposits. The yard was open for a half day on Saturdays so he hung around to help customers load their purchases into their vehicles. He got paid ten bucks for his half day of work.

Chapter 3
Laketown High School

On Monday, the skies were overcast as Mike pedaled his mountain bike to school. He carried his schoolbooks in a backpack strapped to his shoulders atop his khaki jacket. He wore his baseball hat backwards when riding his bike. He turned into the schoolyard and pushed his bike into a slot in a row of racks and then locked it. He headed up the stairs into the two-story building and stopped in front of his locker. He took his brown bag lunch from his backpack and put it into the locker. He took his English literature book out of his pack and tossed it inside the locker. His baseball cap, he tossed in on top of the lit book. He closed the locker door and spun the dial on the lock. He headed down the hall to his math class.

Inside the classroom, he sat down on the desk chair and laid his math book and clipboard on the desktop. He had finished his assignment and felt a little better about trigonometry. He was starting to understand the relationships. He needed trig to satisfy the math requirements of the state's colleges. The teacher kicked off the class work by asking the students to put their homework problem solutions on the classroom whiteboard. Mike was one of those called to the board. The teacher, a middle aged women, Mrs. McConnell, went over all the problems on the board to look for mistakes. Mike's came out correct in all respects. The rest of the hour was spent on a lecture on some new aspects of trig and a new assignment due the next day. Mike thought that he understood the new material. The next hour was his history/social studies class. The class was upstairs. As he trudged up the stairs, he passed one of the girls from the ice rink coming down. He nodded to her and she gave him a half smile in acknowledgement.

History was a good class for Mike. He could relate to the historic characters and their involvements in the events in question. This was European history and it was not a subject that you picked up casually like U.S. History. The big problem here was to remember the sequence of events and their dates. The teacher was a thirtyish man named Mr. Fulton, who seemed at ease with the subject matter. His style of presentation was well suited for the students. Mike was very impressed with the teacher's critique of the actions taken by the historic players. At this point, the class was studying the Roman occupation of the British Isles, as we know them now.

The third class of the morning was Chemistry 2. Mike wasn't too comfortable in this class. The teacher, a Mr. McElroy, didn't like to bog himself down with the slower students. He would just forge ahead and show favoritism for the better students. Mike was probably going to do well enough to just pass this course. He especially didn't like to work with the various acids. Luckily, he worked with a partner in doing the experiments, who was pretty sure of herself. He still didn't memorize all the elements and their valences.

Fourth period came before lunch at Laketown High. Mike welcomed this class since it was Physical Education in which he could play hard and feel relaxed. He would have ordinarily taken swim team for PE, but decided to wait until the spring swim season for the team sport. The reason for this was because of his hockey commitments, which didn't quite blend in with swimming. He liked this class because they ran the mile and commando courses during the week, mixed in with some touch football and soccer. Today was the day they ran the mile around the 400 meter track and did calisthenics. Mike ran a fast 5 1/2 minutes this day, which was his best time ever. He knew he could better it the next week.

After his phys. ed. shower, Mike got dressed and headed for his locker. He grabbed his lunch bag and headed for the lunch area next to the cafeteria. It was still overcast but not raining. He headed for a bench where he spotted a couple of guys on his hockey team. The three skaters high-fived each other and exchanged some post mortems on their recent loss. One of the guys was the center, Jake Hurstmeyer, and the other was the left wingman, Bobby Rockford. Jake was one of team standouts and Bobby was a journeyman puck handler who was still learning.

"I was looking for you guys at the rink last Friday night but didn't see you. I needed the skating practice and so do you guys," he laughed.

"I was kind of disgusted, so I said, 'screw it'," commented Jake.

" Who, me, do I need skating practice?" joked Bobby. "I couldn't get a ride over there, Friday. All the family cars were out and about."

"Well, anyway, I was there," said Mike. "Every little bit helps. Any time you guys need a ride, call me. I get to drive my dad's pickup truck."

"I'm hoping coach can scratch up some more skaters for the team," bemoaned Jake. "We don't even have a full second line. I'm the only true center on the team."

"It ain't gonna be easy," warned Mike. "I didn't see any promising skaters at the local rink, except for the younger hockey players."

※

Two guys walked up to the trio and stopped in front of them. One of them, a tall guy with a crew cut, looked at them.

"Which one of you is Mike Thomas?" he asked.

"I'm Mike," replied Mike after a moment's hesitation.

"I'm Johnny Heller," the tall guy said. "There a rumor going around that you tried to get chummy with my girlfriend the other night at the ice rink."

Mike stood up, and lay his lunch down on the bench.

"Huh. Who's your girlfriend?" replied Mike.

"Her name is Evelyn, a blond who goes to school here."

"And she's your girlfriend?" asked Mike.

"That's right. She's my girlfriend," he stated.

"Who told you I was getting chummy with her?" asked Mike.

"Some of her friends who were at the rink with her," said Johnny Heller.

"You mean that they said I tried to steal her away from you?" asked Mike, pressing on.

"They said you skated with her," he said.

"Did your girlfriend Evelyn tell you I skated with her?" asked Mike.

"No, I haven't talked to her about it yet," said Johnny Heller.

"Well, yeah, I did skate with a girl named Evelyn," admitted Mike. "She came over and asked me to skate with her. Did anyone tell you that?"

"No, not really," said Johnny Heller.

"And this girl Evelyn didn't say shit about being your girlfriend," pressed Mike. "If she belongs to you, she better stay away from other guys. I don't keep track of who owns what girl around here."

"Well, now you know she's my girlfriend so stay away from her," said Johnny Heller.

"I only know what you tell me. This Evelyn didn't think to tell me about you. She only knew I was a good skater and I played hockey," answered Mike. "She came over to me and asked me to skate with her, okay. Maybe next time you should take her skating."

"Just stay away from her," warned Johnny Heller.

"Just tell her to stay away from me, big guy," replied Mike.

At that, the tall kid, Johnny Heller, walked away with his friend. Mike stood watching them leave and then sat down. He picked up his half eaten sandwich and looked at it. The three friends sat quietly for a few moments.

❧

"You know who that guy is?" asked Bobby.

"Not really," replied Mike. "Who is he?"

"He's the big football hero at school here," answered Bobby.

"Do you know him, Jake?" asked Mike.

"Yeah, I know him," replied Jake. "You ought to go to more football games, Mike."

"You think he's gonna pick a fight with a hockey player?" inquired Mike.

"Boy, you defensemen, always looking for a fight," chided Jake, shaking his head.

"Be careful who you skate with at the rink, you guys," cautioned Mike.

⚜

After a time, the bell rang to end the lunch break. It was time to go to fifth period, time for English literature class for Mike. They would be studying about Alfred Lord Tennyson this hour. He kind of liked Alfred Lord Noyes better, the author of "The Charge of the Light Brigade." He picked up and headed for his locker. After that, it was sixth period Spanish language class that he needed to fulfill his college requirements. The Spanish teacher was a Mrs. Spitzer, a good looking brunet who looked to be about forty. It was his 2nd year of Spanish and he was becoming fairly fluent in it. He wasn't sure though, how it would help him out in the business world in later years. Wisconsin was a long way from Puerto Rico and Mexico.

Chapter 4
A New Teammate

The rink at Holcomb's Acres was shaped like a big Quonset hut. Inside, the ice sat between opposite sets of bleachers on the sides, painted white. This made it ideal for the fans watching the game. The dressing rooms were at the back end of the structure. All nine members of the Laketown team were seated on the visitor bench holding their sticks between their legs. The coach was talking to them about game strategy.

"These guys have only lost one game. They're tough. Try to keep them away from the net," he admonished. "You defensemen, don't go for their deeks when they're coming at you. Just stay in front of them till it's time to check 'em. I want the center to lie back a little and let the wings chase the puck. We're going to put up a strong defense. Got it?"

"Yo, coach," responded the skaters.

At that, they got up and skated out on the ice to warm up. The home team came out a few seconds later. They practiced shooting and skating in circles. The referee blew the whistle to line up for the face-off. The ref dropped the puck and the game was on. Laketown defenseman Donny Smith got the puck and passed it out to the right side wingman next to the boards. Elmer Johansen, the wing, dumped the puck across the blue line and the chase was on. The puck eventually came back to Mike at the blue line. He skated it across the line, then passed back to Smith. A shot was taken which was a little wide of the mark and the wings were trying to dig it out behind the net, battling the home team defensemen. When the rival defenseman got hold of the puck, the Laketown skaters scurried back across the red line to set up a defense. This was the plan.

The puck was being carried back and forth and side to side and the game was scoreless deep into the first period. With a minute left, Mike banged the puck to the left side boards of the opposition end and wingmen Bobby Rockford corralled it and passed it back to Mike, who faked a slap shot then passed it off to Smith who slapped it into the net over the goalkeeper's shoulder. A shout went up as the scoring team whooped it up with sticks extended in the air. The score was Laketown 1, Holcomb's Acre 0. Shortly thereafter, the buzzer went off ending the first period. This was a good start for Laketown. They had kept the enemy away from their net with a stout defense. Their coach was smiling when they came back to the bench.

"Well, we won the first period," he exulted. "Same game plan for the next period, guys."

Mike's line stayed on the bench at the beginning of the second period. There were only three defensemen on the team, so he alternated with Donny Smith at times on line changes. The third defenseman was Herb Wisner, a late addition to the team. The action was becoming very intense on the ice, with the home team showing some frustration about being held scoreless. The checking was becoming vicious. When Mike came back out on the ice, there was a lot of shoving and bumping action behind his net with the opposing wingmen fighting over the puck. Late in the period, Mike was fortunate enough to break loose across the blue line and do a one on one with the other goalie. His first shot was blocked and his second on the rebound was smothered. He skated quickly back to his position on the blue line as the other team took possession of the puck. The puck was intercepted by one of the Laketown skaters and got loose in front of the crease. There was a lot of stick action in front of the net and the next thing we know is that the puck ended up in the opponents net. It was another score for the visitors. Bobby Rockford got credit for the goal with no assist established. The celebration was less than enthusiastic. The crowd thought the puck was kicked into the net. The period ended with the score now, Visitors 2, Home team 0.

The action in the third period found the home team becoming very aggressive, fighting for their first score. Mike was cited for roughing and spent two minutes in the penalty box. He was caught for using his forearm across the face of the opponent's wingman. With the visitors short handed, the home team scored their first goal. It was scored by their center after a face-off in front of the Laketown net. The score stood Visitors 2, Home team 1. So far, the Laketown goalkeeper was doing an exemplary job, allowing only one goal. So far Mike was easing up on the hard checking which would please his dad. This behavior on his part was helping to keep him free of extraneous retaliation.

The rest of the period found the teams engulfed in a lot of rock'em, sock'em action back and forth. Finally, a home team wingman got control of a loose puck in front of the Laketown net and put it past the goalie. The score was now tied 2 to 2. The teams had played to a tie. The overtime period would start in ten minutes. The league was playing sudden death overtime. Whoever scored first would be the winner.

The coach decided to start the first line. He didn't want to lose this game. They had fought too hard to take a chance on a quick score by their opponents. He was going to send in substitutes on an individual basis. The opponents got the puck on the face-off. They worked their way into the Laketown zone until Mike took the puck away from their center and moved it up to the opponent's zone. From there, he passed the puck off to Smith. Smith became open for an instant and tried a slap shot. The puck flew wide of the net and the opponents picked it up and moved it to center ice through a series of passes. The left winger, McAdoo, made a quick darting move and took the puck away from the opponent's and skated it across the blue line. He was quickly tied up by the Holcomb defenseman who flipped the puck away to center ice. The puck changed sides this way all through the overtime period.

This is how the game ended. After the buzzer, the opposing teams skated past each other, high-fiving with their gloves. The teams glided back to their benches and sat down, exhausted.

"You guys played a good game," declared coach Joshua. "Too bad we couldn't hold 'em at the end. We stopped their winning streak though. They were probably thinking we would be pushovers."

"We ought to congratulate our goalie, coach," spoke up Sven, one of the centers. "He was blocking just about everything."

"Yeah," cried the team. "Good game goalie."

"Thanks, you guys," answered Tim Blakely, the goalkeeper.

Mike noticed a newcomer, sitting close behind them on the bottom row of the bleachers. It was a girl dressed in a heavy khaki jacket with a hoodie. She didn't look like anybody's sister that he knew about. He looked at her for a few seconds and noticed she wasn't moving around like she was going to leave. Some of the parents in attendance were walking off to the exit point of the rink to wait for their kids.

"Don't leave yet, you guys," said the coach. "I have an important announcement. We have a new player on our team. You know we're kind of short-handed so she's going to help fill out our team."

"She?" thought Mike. "Did I hear right?"

"Come on down here, Mary Jane, and meet your new team," said the coach.

The girl in the khaki jacket got up from her bleacher seat and stepped down to the end of the visitor bench next to coach Joshua.

"This is Mary Jane Evans, guys," said the coach. "She's going to play wingman. She's an experienced hockey player and was playing for a girls' team. Her family just moved here, not here I mean, but Laketown, our town, from Milwaukee. Her dad used to play hockey, too. She's probably too good a skater for our team but we are the only team around. So there you have it, my announcement."

The girl just stood there, quite embarrassed and waved her hand and said "Hi". "I hope I can help out your team," she said.

"Now all we need is one more defenseman and we've got two lines," grinned coach, Joshua.

Mike just sat there stunned. Likewise it was with the rest of the team. Nobody was expecting a girl for a teammate. He looked at the girl standing beside Coach Josh. She had dark brown hair under her hood and she looked to be about 5 foot 7 inches tall or maybe 5'8" at the tallest. Well at least she wasn't undersized. You couldn't tell what her body was like under the jacket. She was wearing some kind of sweat pants so you couldn't see her legs. There was nothing out of the ordinary about her face. She had regular features and strong chin. "Oh well," thought Mike. We'll have to wait until we see her at practice. Some of the guys went up and shook hands with her. Mike wasn't one of them. He followed the others out into the night with his hockey bag and sticks. His dad hadn't come to the game. Mike had come with the center, Jake Hurstmeyer and his mom. Mike jumped into the back seat of the van and buckled up. Jake's mom wheeled them out into the access road and headed back to Laketown. They were about 18 miles from there.

"Well, Michael, what do you think of your new teammate?" inquired Jake's mother.

"Don't ask," begged Mike at the question.

Jake's mom started laughing. She couldn't stop for a full minute.

"Uh," offered Jake. She can't hurt the team that much. Remember, she's not displacing another member.

"Man, it's a good thing she's not a defenseman," muttered Mike. "I hope she doesn't have asthma or something debilitating where they have to give her oxygen."

His comments brought more laughter from Jake and his mother. Mike had played on a bantam team with a girl teammate who had asthma and had to sit down and rest, periodically, throughout the games.

"I don't see how she's going to make our team that much better. She'll probably hang around near the blue line waiting for the puck to come her way," noted Mike, continuing with his dim view assessment.

"She's not bad looking, Mike," said Jake. "I got a close look at her so don't be bitchin' to her if she screws up. You gotta respect good looks."

"Ha, ha, ha," laughed Mike. Don't remind me of good looks. Remember I just got into a scrape with that guy Heller over his "pinup" girlfriend."

"Ha," countered Jake. "What if that dame asks you to skate with her again? You gonna turn her down?"

"I'll tell her to stay away from me. I'm not getting into it again with her boyfriend. Anyway, what am I going to do with her. She's so good looking she scares me. Aaaa, she's not going to mess with me, not if she's got a football hero guy."

"Who is this "pinup" girl, Mike?" asked Jake's mother.

"She's a beautiful girl from school, very popular, that asked me to hold hands with her down at the skating rink, last Friday. I didn't come on to her or anything like that. She thought I was a good skater. That's all," replied Mike.

"Are you dating any of the girls at school?" continued on Jake's mother.

"No soap with that," Mrs. Hurstmeyer. "I haven't got the money to wine and dine 'em."

"How about you, Jake? You've taken some to the show, I know," she commented.

"Nobody serious, Mom," replied Jake.

His mother made a left turn off the highway onto a side road, which led to Laketown. The trio was silent the rest of the way to town. Eventually, she pulled up in front of Mike's house and stopped the car. Mike got out, grabbed his hockey bag and sticks and thanked Jake and his mom for the ride.

"See you in school tomorrow, Mike," called out Jake.

"Right," answered Mike.

❧

He made his way up the short walkway, took out his house key and opened the front door. He started up the stairway, when his dad called out to him.

"How'd you guys do?" asked Dad.

"We tied 2 to 2. I played a good game. Uh, and we got a new player," he added.

"No kidding," asked his dad.

"She's a girl," replied Mike, who opened his bedroom door and went in. He threw his hockey bag on the floor and laid his sticks on top. He sat down on the bed and dropped his head back on to his pillow.

Chapter 5
Swim Team Signup

It was early January and the week of the swim team signups at the high school. Swim team would start practicing starting in February. The hockey season would extend out into early March so there was some overlap. The ground was covered with a thin layer of snow, so swimming seemed somewhat unseasonal. Mike walked into the boy's gym and headed for the coach's office. It was so during the recess break so he thought it was a good time to take care of business. He looked inside and saw the swim coach, Mr. Allison, sitting at a desk. He knocked at the door then turned the doorknob and went in. The coach of the soccer team was sitting at his desk in the far corner of the office. He stepped in front of Mr. Allison's desk and said, "Excuse me, sir". The coach looked up.

"Hi, uh, I'm swimming next semester. Can I sign up?" he asked.

"Where you been, Thomas? You didn't take the swim class this semester," he inquired.

"Couldn't do it coach. I'm playing hockey this season and it wouldn't have worked out for me. Sorry about that," replied Mike. "I did a little swimming over at the "Y", though, so I can still compete."

"Yeah, I know you play hockey so I know you're still in shape," said the coach. "What do you want to concentrate on this season, backstroke again?"

"Backstroke and breaststroke," answered Mike. "I've been working on the breaststroke."

"Well, glad you're coming back, Thomas," said the coach. "We should have a good team this year."

"Do you want me to sign up or something?" asked Mike.

"No, you don't have to sign up. Just elect swim team on next semester's gym class. You're a returnee, so I don't have to interview you or anything like that," said the coach. "I know you're a racer. How are your grades? No problem with them is there?"

"No, I'm good there," assured Mike.

Just then, the bell rang ending the recess period.

"Okay coach, I'll see you then," said Mike, heading for the door.

※

Mike headed for his chemistry class. As he made his way down the hallway he was thinking back to his history class earlier in the morning. He was ready for anything the teacher wanted to throw at him. He was becoming an expert on the rise of the Roman Empire. It seemed like the Romans wanted to reach out and conquer everything in sight. They were fighting barbarians in the British Isles. Those were the good old days, thought Mike. But they didn't play hockey so forget it.

When he sat down, he nodded to Herb Wisner, the extra defenseman, who was also in the class. Wisner was one of the guys in class who always had the right answer. He was into studying. Mike looked around the classroom and saw a new girl sitting up front with her back to him.

"Who the hell is that?" he wondered.

The teacher welcomed the class back, as usual and stood there for a second.

"We have a new student whom will be finishing the semester with us," announced the teacher. "Her name is Mary Jane Evans just to let you know."

The teacher went back to his desk, sat down, and went on with the lesson.

"Mike, Mr. Thomas," he addressed him. "Who was the commander of the Roman invaders in Britain?"

Mike stood up, looked down at his notes and answered, "Aulus Plantius in 43 AD.

"You're right on that Michael," he said. "And who was the Roman Emperor during this invasion?"

"Uh, well, it wasn't Julius Caesar, he had gone to Britannia earlier, about 80 years earlier. It may have been Nero or Caligula or maybe Claudius Augustus, I think," answered Mike, thinking hard.

"Well let's see if anyone else knows the answer to that," said Mr. Fulton. "Mr. Wisner, you've got your hand up. What say you?"

"Tiberius Claudius Caesar Augustus Germanicus, to be exact," replied Herb Wisner.

"Right on, Mr. Wisner, a little before Nero and a little after Caligula," commended the teacher. "You were close on that Michael."

"That Wisner guy has all the answers," Michael muttered to himself. "How can a hockey guy be that smart?"

❧

Chemistry class was still the same old miserable undertaking. Mike stood close by his lab partner as she guided herself through the hydrochloric gas experiment.

"Hey, you got that right, Jennifer?" inquired Mike. "You sure?"

"Of course it's right, partner," she answered. "Trust me."

She had gone over to McElroy and got his thumbs up on the job done and he duly noted that in his class assignment book. Mike felt lucky he had this Jennifer Lundberg dame as a partner. Jennifer was a girl with a slight wave to her blond hair that almost covered her left eye,. She wore glasses with heavy dark frames, which made her look very scholarly. Mike noticed that her legs were nicely shaped.

"You'll go far, Jennifer. What's your major?" lauded Mike. "You're already a chemistry pro."

"Probably medicine. I don't think pharmacy. Whatever. I'll get there," she shrugged.

"Well go for it girl. You've got my vote!" exclaimed Mike.

❧

Mike had a hard time concentrating on Spanish class that afternoon. He was a little excited about swim team next semester. He felt like he was going to score high in all the swim meets. He was particularly focused on his breaststroke practice, which he felt was getting a lot better.

❧

That night the team met at the rink for a hockey practice. The coach wanted to orient the new female wingman into the system. They went through the backward skating exercises in a game like fashion. The new girl handled the backwards moves well enough. She was wearing her old hockey shirt from her old team. Her dark brown hair hung down in strings from her helmet. She looked quite at home on her skates and kept her shoulders back. There were some usual wind sprint sessions and a little bit of scrimmaging between the two lines with the coach playing the part of the missing defenseman on the second line. Mike tried to do a little fancy puck handling during the process. Coach Joshua had to remind him to do a little more passing. Hot-dogging wasn't going to be a steady solution to having a winning season.

It was obvious that the new wingman knew her stuff. She would likely hold up her end of the bargain. Getting into rough going in battling over the puck would be the big question mark for her. She didn't say much during the practice but some of the guys talked to her afterwards. Defenseman Wisner was one of them. Mike hadn't talked to her since she came aboard.

※

After the practice, the team players went into the locker room to change back into their street clothes. When Mary Jane came into the dressing room, she spoke out about just taking off her skates and putting on her shoes to drive home. She sat down, changed into her shoes and took off her shoulder and elbow pads. She wore a tee shirt underneath her pads. She looked to be in pretty good shape. She put on a jacket, picked up her bag and sticks and left. Coach walked her out to her car just to make sure she was safe.

"Getting dressed and undressed could be a little sticky having a girl on the team," said Donny Smith.

"Well, just don't look at her," advised Bobby Rockford, with a chuckle.

Chapter 6
Game at Mapleton

Coach rented a school bus for this game. Mapleton was 40 miles north of Laketown. The weather was kind of snowy late in January. The ride went okay and the ice rink looked well insulated when they pulled up. The players filed out, toting their bags and sticks and entered the building. Only one parent came along for the ride. It was Mary Jane's dad, apparently concerned about how his daughter would fare against the boys. Her dad was a tall guy with light brown hair wearing a foul weather jacket. The skaters finished dressing in the locker room and came out to the visitor's bench. Mary Jane had finished dressing on the bench. The Zamboni was putting the finishing touches on the ice surface. The officials were waiting outside the ice floor leaning against the boards.

The Laketown skaters were stretching their leg muscles before going out on the ice. They all glided out on the ice when the Zamboni made its exit. They skated around in various patterns for a brief spell, then practiced shooting at the net. The opposing team was warming up on the other side of the ice. They wore Chicago Blackhawk style uniforms with the word Mapleton on their shirts. Laketown shirts were fashioned after the Jersey Bluedevils.

When they set up for the face-off, the second line was out with Donny Smith and Herb Wisner as defensemen. Mike Thomas would be on the first team when it took to the ice. The new girl was on the right wing position. The center was Sven Olavson and the other wing, a guy named Randy McAdoo. The goalkeeper, Blakely, was skating nervously in a tight circle. On the face-off, Mapleton controlled the puck. The defensemen took their time passing the puck back and forth, and finally passed to the center at the red line. They worked their way into the Laketown area and the puck ended up on the stick of the left winger. Mary Jane moved in, poking with her stick and shoving the winger from behind. She seemed to be tying him up successfully with her style of play. He twisted around swinging his elbow trying to fend off the girl. She leaned backwards to avoid being struck. Mike wasn't sure that the other team knew they were playing against a female winger. The puck eventually went sliding back and forth between the two teams and until it was taken away by the center, Sven, who took it into Mapleton ice, took a shot that went wide and back of the net where a battle took place between Sven and a defenseman. Several minutes later the first team came out on the ice for a line change with Donny Smith staying in for a second shift.

Mike had been watching the game intently looking for any weakness in the home team's armor. He noticed their center was a hotshot puck hog that tried to score unassisted. He figured the rest of the team wasn't that aggressive. He started off his shift by passing the puck back and forth with Smith, working their way across the enemy blue line. Smith chipped the puck into the backboards and the center Hurstmeyer went after it. He passed it out to Bobby Rockford who passed it back to Hurstmeyer who flipped the puck into the net halfway up the back end. The team whooped it up for a second and patted the center on the helmet. The visitors were ahead 1 – 0. At that, the second line came out for their shift. Mike stayed in with Wisner replacing Smith. The puck changed hands for a long time in the first period, with the skaters digging back and forth to attack and defend. The buzzer sounded ending the first period with the score one to nothing. So far, Mike hadn't checked anybody violently as yet. On the defense side of the coin, the Laketown goalie had been pretty well protected.

"Okay guys, you held them pretty well," declared the coach. "Next period let's take a few more shots. You wingers sneak in front of the net area whenever you can and take some shots, good or bad. We gotta score some goals. Mary Jane, you don't have to grapple with their guys so much. As soon as they skate away from the boards with the puck, start poking at the puck and their stick. You have to do a lot of back skating."

"Okay coach," she nodded. "Will do."

"And Wisner, let's take a few slap shots," he instructed. "You're getting open, I noticed. Don't let Mike do all the shooting."

The buzzer sounded for the 2nd period. The second line took to the ice first. Smith went in at defense. Laketown got control of the puck on the face-off and Olavson flipped it into the enemy zone and the team gave chase. Smith and Wisner stopped at the blue line and kept batting the puck toward the net. After a few chases back and forth, Laketown got the puck back. Wisner skated it inward and backhanded it to the wing on his side of the net. There was scramble for the puck and the Laketown winger backhanded the puck toward the net where it caromed off the goalie's stick and into the net and the red light went on as the ref signaled a goal with his left hand. Goal scored and it's now 2 to nothing, visitors. And guess what, Mary Jane Evans scored the goal and Wisner the assist. The coach's strategy worked. On the line change, coach shook her hand when she sat down.

Mike was back on the ice with Smith. The Mapletons were getting frustrated and started checking harder and battling for the puck. Their center was trying to brute force the puck into the net and was pushing hard on Mike. Mike kept his stick on their center's stick to prevent him getting a shot off. He eventually slapped the puck off the right side boards and across the enemy blue line. Hurstmeyer got control and skated the puck around behind the net and forced it up and around the post for a goal. Again the red light went on, signaling three to nothing for the visitors. After a brief ballyhoo in celebration of the goal, coach sent out the second line for a change. On the way out, Mike took out his mouthpiece and skated up to the girl coming out.

"Listen, they're gonna be checking hard, so use your hands to push off the guy," cautioned Mike. "Don't let 'em hit you hard!"

She nodded back to him. Those were the first words he ever said to her. When they set up for the face-off, Herb Wisner gave her a friendly tap with his stick. With a three goal advantage, the Laketowners were trying to just keep the puck out of their zone for the most part, playing defensively. There were several penalties called with the rough going. The second period ended without any more goals with the score 3 – 0, visitors.

Third period started with the Laketown first line on the ice. The Mapleton team was expecting the visitors to play conservatively since they were far ahead. When the puck came to Mike, he passed it off to Smith who passed it back to him for a time. Mike was maneuvering around in his own zone when the Mapleton center came up fast to try to steal the puck. Mike slapped the puck sideways to the boards, skated around the center, raced forward, and retrieved the puck and hightailed it to the enemy goal. He got by the defenseman, deeked once to the right, then flipped the puck past the goalie into the net. The red light went on, visitors 4, home team zero. Mike got a cheer from his teammates and raised his stick in the air. It wasn't an incidental goal by chance. Mike had planned it when the opponents became overly aggressive. The game ended with a 4 to zero victory for Laketown. On the post game handshake skateby, the home team seemed to be in a state of shock. Mike said, "Nice game" to their center.

The team changed from their skates into their shoes and hurried out to the bus, lugging their bags, not wanting to unwind in the dressing room. Once they were seated, the coach stood up in the front of the bus and congratulated the team. He reminded them that the next game would be a home game and to tell the folks to come on out to cheer them on. The winger, Mary Jane, was talking to her dad and smiling. She got a goal in her first game. On the way home, her dad got up and leaned over to Mike.

"My daughter said you helped her," he said. "Thanks."

"No problem," Mike answered. "She did good."

It was Saturday night. Mike was planning to sleep late the next morning. There was a lot of chatter on the bus on the way back home.

Chapter 7
Back Home at Home

Coach dropped the kids off at their homes. Herb Wisner was one of the first teammates let off the bus. He stepped carefully through the light layer of snow covering his walkway. He wiped his feet off on the doormat, opened the front door with his key and went inside. He was met at the door by the family dog, an English Setter. He stroked the dog quickly with his free hand and laid his hockey bag and sticks down.

"Anyone home?" he called out.

It was Saturday night and his parents might have gone out. The light was on in the kitchen and found his younger sister and her friend sitting at the table working on their laptop computers. His sister looked up and waved at him. She was a tenth grader at the high school.

"Mom and Dad gone out?" he asked.

"They went to the show," she replied. "About 2 hours ago."

"What's playing?" he asked.

"Ten minutes to nowhere," she joked. "I don't know."

"What are you girls doing, homework, ha, ha?"

"Did you guys have a game?" she asked.

"Yeah, we won," he answered.

"Did they let you play?" she continued.

"Of course I played," he retorted. "We change lines every three minutes."

"How many lines are there?" she asked.

"Two lines, actually we're short handed," he said.

"Oh," she said.

Herb went to the refrigerator and took out a soda. He looked closer for something to eat. He took out what looked like a pot of mixed vegetables and put it on the stovetop. He turned on the burner and looked closer into the refrigerator. He took out two slices of bread and a package of sliced cheese and went to work making a sandwich. He heard the front door open. It was undoubtedly his parents.

"Look out for my bag," he called out. "Don't trip on it."

"Ah, you're home," answered his dad. "How'd the game go?"

"Surprise. We shut 'em out, four to nothing," replied Herb.

"Geez, you must have been busy playing defense," commented his dad.

"We've only got three defensemen. We're pretty good, I'm thinking," explained Herb.

"Who got the goals?" continued his dad.

"Well, Thomas got the fourth one. A couple of the wings and maybe the center got the other three. The new girl on the wing got one and I got the assist."

"The girl, huh?" asked his dad. "Is she any good?"

"She seems okay," said Herb. "We were worried she'd get hurt by all the checking. She's in my History, AP class."

"You got a girl on your team? You better check her hormone count or DNA or something," interjected his sister.

"Nah, she's a good looking girl," exclaimed Herb.

Herb's sister's girlfriend got up with her laptop.

"If you're going to hash over a hockey game all night, I'm gonna head on home," said his sister's friend.

"Just a minute, Laura," said Herb's dad. "Herb will walk you home. It's already dark."

"So long, Betty Lou. See you Monday in school," said friend Laura.

"G'nite," replied Betty Lou. "What'ya doing tomorrow?"

"Eh, going to Church, and I dunno," Laura replied.

"Take a jacket, Herbert," said Herb's mother Wilma. "And take the dog with you."

Wilma was from South Carolina. She had met up with husband, Arnold, when he was a student at the Citadel in Charleston. Herb grabbed his jacket, put the leash on the dog, and followed Laura out the door. She lived a block away. It had stopped snowing.

❦

When Mike got off the bus, he saw his dad's truck and mom's SUV parked in the driveway. He guessed they were staying home tonight. He toted his bag and sticks up to the door. He stopped for a moment looking for his house key in his hockey bag. He found it in the front pocket of his khaki pants. He let himself in and carried his hockey gear to the hall closet. He left the bag zipper open to let it air out. He was still wearing his hockey uniform as he climbed the stairs to his room.

"Is that you, Mike?" his mom called out.

"Yeah, yeah," he answered.

"You okay?" she inquired.

"Yeah, I'm okay. I'm going to shower."

It was Saturday night but he wasn't planning to go out. He undressed and took his towel wrapped around him to the bathroom. After he showered he put on a pair of cargo shorts, a tee shirt, and sandals and went down to the kitchen. His mom and dad were there, watching a cable news show on the TV.

"Well, how did the game go in Mapleton?" asked his dad.

"We skunked 'em," replied Mike. "Four to nothing. Coach had a good game plan that worked."

"You guys must have had a good time coming back on the bus?" opined his dad.

"Yeah, we were feeling good about the game," conceded Mike, "Anything left to eat?"

"No, we thought maybe you could skip dinner tonight," laughed his mother.

"That's okay with me," Mike said. "Are we trying to lose weight or save money?"

"We've got beans and potatoes on the stove and you can make a salad," said his mom.

"No meat, huh?" asked Mike.

"We think that you don't have to eat meat every meal," answered his mom. "We've been reading up on the subject."

"I'm graduating in June," commented Mike, when he sat down with his dinner plate. "I'm trying to decide where to go to college. If I stay in Wisconsin, I might save on tuition."

"You going to play hockey in college?" inquired his dad.

"Yeah, I guess so. It might help me get a scholarship. If I join the ROTC that'll be another break, maybe."

"Well that's a bit of news," replied his dad. "You could end up in the army, afterwards. Did you think about that?"

"You going to go into the army after college?" asked his mom, with raised eyebrows.

"Maybe," replied Mike. "I haven't got any concrete plans right now. I'm going to major in economics or finance, I think. With that I can go on to law school, too."

"You better get busy looking for the school you'll apply to," said his dad. "They want your application ahead of time, you know."

"What's Angie gonna do after she gets her degree?" asked Mike.

"Her major is related to some medical technology," replied Dad. "She'll get into something big, I'm sure. And maybe grad school."

"Good beans, mom," Mike complimented her.

"You're very welcome, thank you," she replied.

"I'll look at some of the schools around the state, Dad. I'll check 'em out on the Internet."

"You do that," said Dad.

∽

Mary Jane Evans and her dad climbed the short flight of stairs leading into their apartment building. Her dad held her sticks and she carried the bag. They had moved into town a month before and were looking for a house to rent. Her dad was a branch manager for a Savings and Loan company who had recently been transferred from Milwaukee to Laketown. Her mother was a freelance bookkeeper. Both of her parents were one-time athletes, so approved of her playing hockey. They entered their apartment on the first floor. It was a two-bedroom unit with one and a half bathrooms. She shared a bedroom with her younger sister. Her mother and sister were at home sitting in the kitchen.

"Oh, good, your home," exclaimed her mother. "It was a long ride wasn't it?"

"Oh, that it was," replied her father. "But the time went by fast. Her team won."

"How did you like playing with boys?" asked her sister.

"It was an experience," replied Mary Jane. "They play a little faster than I'm used to but I stayed with it. Let me put my bag away and I'll be right back."

The mother, who's name was Carol, turned to her husband and asked,

"How did she do Fred? I'm sure you were watching her closely."

"Well, first of all, she scored a goal. That was something. I don't know, though. Those guys play rough. She's going to have to learn how to protect herself better. We don't want her to get injured. The team needs her. They're shorthanded."

"Let her play," shrugged her dad, after a short pause. "If things get too rough for her, she can drop out."

Mary Jane wandered back into the kitchen and sat down.

"I'm going to eat oatmeal, I think. I don't want to eat a big meal," she said.

"You want to stay on the team, Janie?" asked her mother.

"I guess so. They have no girls' team here. I'll have to stay."

"Have you got any homework?" asked her dad. "You're in two AP classes. You've got to study a lot."

"Yes, I'll do it. I just want to sit a while and relax. Two of my teammates are in my European History class. I'm impressed. They must be high achievers. So two of the skaters on my team are good students."

"Oh, that's another thing. Did you send in your application to the university?" asked her mother. Her parents were strong advocates for college, whatever your interests.

"Yes, I did, for sure," she replied. I sent one to U of W in Madison and one to Lakeland University in Plymouth.

"What's the tuition at Lakeland?" asked her dad. "Near Sheboygan, right?"

"It's $24,000, I think. It's private," she replied. "U of W is expensive."

Chapter 8
Hockey Practice

The dressing room in Laketown was crowded with hockey players. It was practice night, Wednesday, for three of the teams. The Bantams were on the way out and the Midgets were on the ice next. The Pee Wees were on the ice the first hour.

"Let's move your butts out of here, you Bantam teeny-boppers and make room for the Midgets!" called out Bobby Rockford.

"Aw, go fly a kite, Midget flip," retorted one of the Bantams. "We just got off the ice!"

"We need a lot of space, okay, so hurry up and put on your overalls," came back Bobby."

"Go put on your sister's underwear, Rocky!" sounded the comeback. "Ha, ha."

"Thank God we got you for a spokesman, Bobby," chimed in Jake Hurstmeyer. "Or else we'd be in big trouble."

The Midgets were dressed in their practice shirts for practice sessions. When they were all suited up, they trudged out and went out onto the ice. The Zamboni machine was making its last row of ice before exiting. The coach threw out a handful of pucks for shooting practice. Some of the skaters were doing their stretching movements. The bleachers were empty except for a few of the parents and some neighbor kids. The players were taking turns flipping the puck toward the net. The goalkeeper, Blakely, was in the crease knocking away the shots. A few minutes later, Mary Jane and her dad were walking down the padded pathway. She took off her skate guards and stepped onto the ice. Her dad climbed up a couple of bleacher rows and sat down to watch the goings on.

"Okay you guys, start skating around the rink, forwards and backwards," called out the coach. "Let's go as fast as you can, like we're in a game."

A few moments later, he had them skating up and down the ice in pairs passing the puck back and forth on the way. They shot into the net at end of each run.

"Now let's line up the two teams for a scrimmage!," hollered the coach. "Mike, you be the lone defenseman on Olavson's line. Smitty, you and Wisner team up on the first line." There was no goalkeeper in one of the nets. Coach had Blakely switching nets every ten minutes or so.

Coach tossed the puck into the middle of the ice and the teams went at it. Whenever Mike started to zig-zag around with the puck, coach yelled, "Let's be passing more!" It was obvious this would be a passing oriented practice..

"And take it easy on the checking," he added. "No use you guys getting injured in practice."

A lot of this, Mike thought, had to do with having a girl in the mix. The coach wanted her to build up her confidence. As it was, it looked like she knew how to play her position. He would pass up to her and have her pass back to him when she was hemmed in, that or knock it back of the opponents net. She kept after the puck whenever she thought it was necessary.

Mike noticed that whenever Mary Jane skated up with the puck, Wisner just poked his stick around at the puck and didn't put a shoulder into her. Well, coach told us not to bang into each other, he remembered. It was a strange picture to see the one defenseman, Mike, on the blue line skating back and forth with out having another defenseman with whom to pass. As it turned out, it was a good practice with passing as the objective.

After 30 or 40 minutes, coach called a halt to the scrimmage. The players skated around cooling off for a while.

"Everybody to the far side of the rink and line up for wind sprints," called out the coach.

This was the routine windup of the practice. After the wind sprints, the skaters would be gasping for air. The teammates slowly glided to the far end of the ice and got into their ready stances. The sprints would go back and forth from end to end.

"Go," shouted the coach at the beginning of each sprint. By the third or fourth heat, the guys would be slowing down, not caring to make a race of it. The best skaters usually led the pack. The goalie, with all his padding, and required to participate, would bring up the rear.

"Now backwards, this time!" the coach shouted.

After two of those, the practice ended. The skaters labored to the open exit and sat down on the bleacher seats. Mary Jane's dad quietly mentioned to his daughter after she sat down, "I got tired just watching."

"How did it go, Wisner, defending the girl," Mike asked the other defenseman.

"Not so bad," replied Wisner. "She's a pretty good stick handler. I'm glad coach said, 'Don't bang on each other'. I didn't want to hurt her."

"I think this practice was good for her." Mike said.

On the way to the dressing room, Wisner went up to Mary Jane and her father and had words with them.

"How'd it go?" asked Wisner of the girl.

"I'm kind of tired," she confessed.

"That's the way we practice," Wisner replied. "We get tired," he laughed.

"This is my dad, Herb," Mary Jane introduced her father. "He played hockey, too."

"My name is Fred," he said shaking hands. "Nice meeting you."

"You too," responded Wisner.

Wisner had his helmet off. His blond hair was dark and matted against his forehead and scalp. He kept looking at Mary Jane. Her eyes looked green or hazel. He liked her smile.

"How do you like AP History?" asked Wisner.

"I like it a lot," she replied. "I was surprised to see you and Mike in the class. I didn't think hockey players were high achievers.

"We're driven, Mike and I," he answered. "We're both looking to go to college. How did you know my name was Herb?"

"I heard some of the guys talking," she replied.

"Just call me Herb," he assured her. "My dad picked out my name and my mom picked out my sister's name ... Betty Lou. My mom's from the south. I don't like the name Herbert all that much"

"Where's your dad from?" she asked.

"He's from Philadelphia. He went to college at the Citadel in Charleston.

"We're kind of native Wisconsinites, huh Dad?"

Her dad nodded affirmatively.

"I gotta go get changed," said Wisner. "See you in school."

Wisner waved goodbye and trudged in his skates to the dressing room. Most of the guys were already dressed and combing their hair. He took off his uniform and pads, took a towel out of his bag and wiped off his body. When he was all dressed he sat down on a bench and waited. He was waiting for Smitty for a ride home.

"See you guys tomorrow," called out Mike. "We gotta get together, Wisner, to bone up on European History, okay?"

"You got that right," replied Wisner. "You're the guru."

"Ha, ha, ha," laughed Mike.

Chapter 9
Working at the Rink

"Hey Mom, guess what?" I'm going to get a part time job," announced Mike.

Mike's mom looked up from the drawer she was fixing in the kitchen.

"You're working Saturdays at the yard," she told him. "You got time for extra work?"

"No, I mean I'm going to have to make some extra money. Ten bucks isn't enough for me. The ten bucks is just coming out of the profits. It's better if I bring in some outside money," he explained.

"Where you going to work?" she inquired.

"I don't know yet but I have some ideas. It should work out good for me. I can still work at the yard on Saturday if things work out right."

"Huh." Muttered his mom. "Well okay. Okay with me. Okay with your dad, probably. Maybe I should spend more time at the yard. That would take the load off of him. He wouldn't have to hire more help this summer."

❧

On the next Friday after school, Mike pedaled his bike over to the ice rink. He rolled the bike in the entranceway and leaned it against the wall. He walked over to the skate shop where he heard the blade sharpener buzzing. The manager, Ernie Strauss, was sharpening skates for the night's skating session. Mike knocked on the inside wall to get his attention.

Ernie turned his head, turned off the grinder and said, "We ain't open for skating yet, Skates. What can I do for you?"

"Hi Ernie," said Mike. This is something else. I need a job, part time. You got anything open?"

Ernie quickly replied, "Yeah, Friday nights. I need someone to work the skate rental counter. That's what I got. How does that sound?"

"I'm your guy, Ernie. Friday nights are perfect for me. I'll take it if you're offering?"

"Okay, be here at 6:30 …. tonight. And you'll probably have to do the Zamboni," instructed Ernie.

"Drive the Zamboni?" asked Mike. "That's sounds even better."

"Be here for sure," added Ernie.

✌

When Mike got home, he strode into the house and looked around for his mom. She was standing over the stovetop making dinner. Mike walked into the room, sat down at the table.

"Mom, I got that part time job. I'll be working Friday nights over at the rink. How does that sound?"

"What cha gonna do, give skating lessons?" she asked, a little surprised by the news.

"Nah, ha, ha," laughed Mike. "I'll be working the skate rental counter."

"How much are they going to pay you?" she asked, intently.

"Oh, I don't even know. I didn't even ask. Huh," answered Mike, sheepishly. "It doesn't really matter. Whatever it is, I don't care."

His mother came over and sat down at the table with him. Her blond hair was a little in disarray, but she still looked beautiful. She still had her shape and good posture. She was wearing blue jeans and an old sweatshirt and a pair of hiking shoes she got at the BIG 5 store.

"You're a 'go-getter', Mike. "That's good. I'm proud of you."

"Thanks, Mom," responded Mike. "I'm proud of you too."

∽

Mike parked his dad's pickup truck at the outermost section of the rink's parking lot. He walked briskly to the entranceway and went inside. He found Ernie in the back office and said, "I'm ready." It was 6:00 PM, a little early.

"Let's go over to the rental counter, Skates, and I'll show you what's what," said Ernie.

He showed Mike where to put the skates after they were returned and told him how to handle the register and the money.

"It's not a big problem, this handling of the skates. They're all arranged by size in their cubbyholes. Don't give out any without payment. Don't take any checks. If they give you a debit or credit card, direct them to the ATM machine where they can take out cash. It's a cash only operation. Got that? And don't be doing anyone a favor. They have to pay in advance. Period. That's four bucks a pair."

"Okay Ernie, I get it," said Mike.

"I'll take you out on the Zamboni when I make first ice and teach you how to operate it," added Ernie.

At 6:30, Ernie started the Zamboni and drove it out of the small corner garage. Mike opened up the side panels of the rink and Ernie brought it out onto the ice.

"Hop on Skates and sit down in the driver's seat. You step on the gas pedal to make it go and press down on this handle to drop water. This stick is for shifting gears, forward and back. Okay let's go. Be careful you don't bump the side panels. You'll be an expert at this in no time at all. You drive in circles around the outer edges and then cut down the center to the other end then start a new row and around the center row that you cut through before. I'll watch you go."

Mike sat down and started his run watching the sides closely near the side panels.

"I'll tell you when to hit the water handle. Just keep going," directed Ernie.

Mike went around and through in good fashion and hit the water drop whenever Ernie shouted to him. At the end of the run, Mike steered the vehicle to the open panels dropped the loose ice in the corner. Ernie took over then and told him to watch as he slowly drove the Zamboni into the small holding room.

Ernie looked almost athletic as he hopped off the machine. For a guy with a heavy torso like his, he was pretty agile. Ernie picked up a shovel and tossed the loose ice onto the drive out floor. Afterwards, they put the side panels back in place and together walked over to the skate counter and went inside.

"You ready?" asked Ernie. "I'll work with you for a while till you get the rhythm."

"I'm ready," replied Mike, nervously.

The doorman opened the doors at 7:00 PM, began collecting the admission fees from the early arrivals. There was no snack bar in the rink. It had been closed down two years before in favor of vending machines.

Mike checked the cash register to see if he had money to make change. He did. He wasn't sure of how to record all the rentals so he got a piece of paper and a pen and marked a one for every pair of skates he rented. He was sure to put the money into the register slots. And so went the night. After an hour of skating, the music stopped and the skaters came off the ice. Ernie pulled the Zamboni out and resurfaced the ice. Afterwards, the music started and the skaters went back on the ice. During the break some of the crowd were returning their rental skates. Mike took the time to put them into the proper cubbyholes. About 9:15, a girl came up and leaned on the counter.

"You're from the high school aren't you?" she asked smiling.

"Uh huh," answered Mike, nodding.

"Hi, I'm Gloria," she said. "I've seen you wandering around the school. I've never seen you working here before."

"I just started, recently," replied Mike.

"What grade are you in?" she further inquired.

"I'm a senior," he answered.

"What time do you get off," she asked.

"Oh boy," Mike thought to himself. "She wants to start up with me. She's not bad looking but I ain't getting involved tonight."

"Oh, not till real late," he said.

"I'm here alone," she said. "Maybe we can meet and do something, you know, no school tomorrow?"

"What grade are you in?" asked Mike.

"I'm in the eleventh," she said.

"Well, maybe we'll see each other in school," he told her. "I've got get back to work," he said, picking up a pair of skates to put away. When he turned back to the counter, the girl Gloria was gone.

The rink closed at 11:00 PM. Mike counted the money in the register. There was $299 in the register. He had counted $35.00 change money when the evening started. That meant he had taken in $264 in rentals. That computed out to 66 pairs rented. He looked at his tab sheet. It added up to 65 units. He had missed one pair, apparently. He wrote the amount of money he had taken in on his piece of paper. He decided, this was a big crowd. Some of the skaters bring their own skates and don't have to rent them.

He waited until Ernie came into the rental room. It was about 11:10 PM when he appeared. Ernie took the money out and put it into a bank bag. He turned to Mike and said, "Come into the office and fill out a W-2 form before you leave, Skates. You're officially on the payroll."

Mike left the rink at about 11:30 and walked to his pickup truck. When he reached the truck he heard a car pull up behind him. He turned around and saw it was the girl Gloria with her driver's side window open. The car was an older model Toyota Corolla.

Mike looked at her for a moment. "Now what?" he thought to himself. "I'd better get rid of her pronto!"

"Good night, Gloria," he waved to her. He got into his truck and closed the door. He started the engine and pulled away. After a leaving the lot, he looked back to see if she was following him. He didn't want her knowing where he lived. So far she wasn't. He decided to drive around and detour for a while in case she was following him. Eventually he made it home and went into the house.

His dad was still up, watching the military channel showing a video about World War II. Mike sat down next to him on the living room sofa.

"Better get to bed, Mike, if you're coming to the yard tomorrow."

"Okay, Dad," Mike replied. "In a few minutes. I have to relax a minute. It was a busy night at the rink."

"What are they paying you, Mike?" asked his dad.

"Twenty-five bucks for the night," he said. "Is that enough."

"That's good, Mike. Save your money. Now get to bed."

"Yo," replied Mike as he got up and went up the stairs.

∽

Mike brushed his teeth, undressed, and got into bed. He thought back about this night's events. He wondered about rejecting a girl who was essentially throwing herself at him. Was he a fool for snubbing her? What was he worried about, getting involved with a girl from school? He had had an intimate relationship the previous year with a girl from the swim team. She was a senior at the time and was now long gone. But at the time, this relationship was suspect by the other swimmers and could have turned into a big problem for him and the girl. He was only 16 at the time. If he had taken up with the girl from the rink tonight, she may have told her friends about it and it and it would be known all over the campus. It could have become an embarrassment for him. Well, at least he didn't have to worry about tonight's encounter. Well, so much for that. What had his mother told him about girls?

She cautioned him, "not to get involved with any girls you're not in love with." Good advice.

Chapter 10
Home Game

Herb Wisner pulled his game shirt over his shoulder pads. He reached into his bag to retrieve his gloves. He put on his gloves and leaned sideways to grab his sticks.

"What's that little tube thing on your chain?" asked Bobby Rockford sitting next to him."

"It's called a Chai," he replied. "My dad asked me to wear it for good luck. It's a Jewish ornament. My dad is Jewish. A lot of guys wear 'em."

"You a Jew, Wisner?" asked Bobby.

"Yeah, kind of," he replied. "My mom's not Jewish. I'm kind of half and half."

"Hey, you're a Jew playing ice hockey!" exclaimed Bobby. "I didn't know Jews played hockey!"

"Now you know, Rockford," stated Wisner, putting on his helmet. "You learn something new every day."

"I played Pee Wee with a couple of Jewish kids," piped in Jake Hurstmeyer. "It's no big deal."

"I saw your dad at one of the games," interjected Bobby. "He just looked like a regular guy."

"He is a regular guy," replied Wisner. "He was in the army in Iraq during 'Operation Enduring Freedom'."

Coach Steenberg came into the dressing room.

"Let's go you guys," he called to them. "We have to warm up. C'mon."

The teammates trudged out of the dressing room out into the rink area and glided off onto the ice. The bleachers on the visitor side of the rink, was dotted with small groups of people supporting the team from Deerfield Creek. The home team stands were filled with family and friends. After the warm up drills, the Laketown Midgets climbed onto the team bench and sat down. Coach was looking out on the ice watching the Zamboni make ice.

After the Zamboni finished its job, the rink was ready for the action ahead. The teams skated out on the ice and did their warm up activities. Blakely, the team's goalkeeper, blocked every practice shot thrown at him. That was a good sign for the coach. When they came back to the bench before the face-off, Wisner sat down next to Mary Jane.

"How you doing?" he asked.

"I'm okay," she replied.

"Be on your toes out there," he advised her. "Don't get clobbered."

"I will, I will," she assured him. "I mean I won't," she added.

❧

Mike's line would start the game. It was he and Smitty at defense, Rockford and Johansen at forward, and Jake Hurstmeyer at center. The Deerfield team controlled the puck after the face-off. The defensemen circled around looking for an opening and passed the puck back and forth for a time then passed to a wing on the red line. They crossed the blue line but quickly lost the puck to Jake, who passed back to Smitty and then they battled their way across the Deerfield blue line. After a short time, the puck ended up behind the Deerfield net where their defenseman battled Rockford for it against the boards.

After a bit of a scuffle the visitors carried the puck into Laketown territory, thusly, back and forth went the puck. The game remained scoreless through most of the period.

With five minutes remaining in the first period, Smitty passed the puck in to Johansen, who took a shot that hit the frame of the net and went bouncing off to the right. Rockford picked it up on his stick, saw Jake in front of the net and passed it to him. Without any maneuvering at all, Jake shot backhanded with his back to the goalie and put the puck into the net for a goal. A big cheer from the crowd went up. Following the usual routine, Jake raised his stick up into the air in celebration. His teammates slapped him on the helmet in accordance. The score was one - nothing, favor of the home team. The first period ended without any more scoring.

Mike looked over his shoulder up at the bleachers looking for his mom or dad. He wanted his dad to watch him play, since he was his best source of feedback on his performance. At first glance he didn't see him. Maybe he was still at the lumberyard locking up the place for the Sunday shutdown. He did see some of the other parents in the bleachers.

"Now pay attention, you guys," said the Coach. "You're looking good so far but I want you centers to hound their defensemen. We have to get on the puck and score more goals. One nothing isn't a big lead, you know."

"Coach, can us defensemen take some slap shots?" asked Donny Smith.

"My answer to that is sure if you've got a clear shot," answered the coach.

After the Zamboni made another round around the rink, the buzzer sounded for the 2nd period. The second line took to the ice. It was Mike's turn to play defense with Wisner. After the face-off, the puck was mostly going back and forth with a lot of stick handling and losing the puck in the middle of the rink. Four minutes into the period, Mike, who had stayed on the ice with the first line, brought the puck out to the Deerfield blue line, passed the puck to Bobby Rockford, then skated into the middle and took a quick pass from Rockford in return. He took the puck to the left of the net, and then he backhanded the puck into the net.

The red light went on and with that, celebration. Mike raised his stick into the air in triumph and bowed to the bleacher crowd. The visiting team's goalie just skated around the crease in a circle in disgust. The score now was two nothing. A moment later, the coach changed lines. Smitty came out to play defense with Wisner and Mike sat down. On the face-off, the game started to get a little rougher with some heated up checking. The puck went into the right corner where it was chased down by Mary Jane. She got to the puck and after a few seconds of jockeying around with it, passed it back to Wisner. A few seconds after she got rid of the puck, she was checked hard into the boards by one of the visitor wingmen. She fell down on the ice. Wisner took a quick flip shot at the net, then took off after the wingman who checked her. He brought his stick up, shoved it crosswise into the guy's chest, and then slugged him with his right hand. The referee, standing right behind Wisner, blew his whistle and called a halt to the play. He pulled Wisner away from the startled victim of the attack and cited him with a major penalty. He skated to the official sitting at a table and made it official, a five-minute penalty for fighting. Wisner went into the penalty box and sat down.

Coach Joshua shook his head and called for a line change. They were now shorthanded.

"I want Mike and Smitty and Jake and Rockford!" he yelled to them intently. "Keep icing the puck, guys."

With the visitors mostly controlling the puck, Mike and Smitty spent a lot of time in the corners fighting for the puck and banging it out whenever they could. When the puck was cleared out to the other end, only Jake chased after it. Rockford stayed back in a defensive mode. It seemed like an eternity, being shorthanded. At one point, the visitors were flooding the ice in front of the Laketown net with their wingmen and center. Eventually, a wingman got an open shot and put it into the net underneath Blakely's stick and the goal and the ref signaled goal. The score was now two to one, home team. It was only about three minutes into the penalty time and the home-towners were still shorthanded. An opponent goal during a major penalty does not cut short the penalty time. There was still two-minutes left before the penalty was over.

The face-off resulted in the Deerfielders mainly controlling the puck and putting heavy pressure on the Laketown skaters. Coach Josh left the first line on the ice in this situation. After another minute, he sent in Sven Olavson to take over for Jake who was getting too tired to chase the puck on icings. The final minute being short handed, was going to be tough for Laketown. Mike and Smitty were getting worn down fighting for the puck in the corners. The puck came out to the visitor left defenseman who quickly fired it into the direction of the net. The was knocked out to the right side of the ice where a Deerfield wingman took a quick shot which was picked up by their center after it was blocked. Finally, the center faked a shot then banged it into the net over Blakely's shoulder. The red light lit up and the Deerfield team celebrated their good fortune with some quick high-fiving. The score was now tied two-two. After a few more seconds, Wisner came skating out on the ice, his penalty over. A few minutes later the period came to an end.

The bench was quiet during the rest period. Some of the players were looking down at their stick blades.

Finally, the coach told them to take a few breaths and relax.

"Okay guy," he said. "It'll be just like starting over. The other team is all charged up with their two goals while they had the advantage. Just play your game with you centers harassing them. Okay."

The third period started out slowly. The second line was back on the ice with Donny Smith partnering with Wisner. The puck was changing hands without too many shots being taken. It seemed the goalies were getting stronger and the skaters running out of gas. All the shots were being blocked or going off target. When the first line was on the ice, Mike took a couple of slap shots which both missed the mark. When time ran out the game ended all tied up two-two. The overtime was cancelled out in the interest of expediency. It was time for the next game to start and there was not sufficient time for another period.

The two teams traded high-fives as they skated on past each other. Then they skated off and headed to their dressing room. Some of the folks in the bleachers followed them in. The Zamboni motor could be heard firing up to make ice for the next game.

"We shoulda won that game," squawked Bobby Rockford as he threw his gloves down. He pulled off his shirt and shoulder pads at the same time and sat down.

"That was my fault," muttered Wisner to Jake Hurstmeyer, sitting next to him. "That five-minute penalty gave 'em their goals."

"Yeah, you got that right," replied Hurstmeyer. "You gotta watch your temper out there."

"Yeah, I know," said Wisner. "I just didn't like that cheap shot move he made on Evans. She didn't even have the puck!"

"Hey, man, this is a cheap shot game," replied Hurstmeyer. "What'aya think, man? She came out of it okay."

∽

Mike was sitting next to his dad, who had followed him in. His mom wasn't there.

"Did mom come?" he asked.

"She's still up in the stands talking to some people," answered his dad. "You played your ass off out there. I was impressed. Blakely really looked good, better in every game. The guy's a great athlete."

"Yeah, he could have shut 'em out, if we weren't that shorthanded," answered Mike.

Coach Joshua got came in and commended the team.

"You guys were almost perfect out there," he said. "We just had a little bad luck. Be sure and come to practice tomorrow at seven PM. We still got more games to play. Let's win 'em all."

The Laketown skaters made their way out of the dressing room, a few at a time. There was a bantam game getting ready to start. Some of the Midgets climbed up into the stands to watch the bantams. Mike and his dad collected his mom and they headed out to the pickup truck in the parking lot. Wisner and Jake walked out to Jake's car for the ride home.

"I got a lot of homework to finish before Monday," said Wisner.

"Yeah, me too," uttered Jake. "You've got AP classes, huh?"

"Yeah, I'm aiming high," he laughed.

"Ya know, that Evans dame ain't a bad player, but the Midgets play rough," said Jake.

"I guess I don't want her to get hurt," said Wisner.

"Well, let's hit the road," said Jake, as they threw their bags and sticks into the back seat of his car.

Chapter 11
Spring Semester

It was snowing hard on that early February morning at the start of the new semester. Mike got a ride with his dad to the high school in the lumberyard pickup. He headed to the school auditorium to establish his class schedule for his last semester. The auditorium was packed with students. Mike spotted Herb Wisner standing at the senior signup station.

"What'a ya think, Wisner?" he asked him as he approached. "You see any AP classes we should get into?"

"Hey, Mike, good seeing you here. It'll help me decide," replied Wisner.

"I gotta take calculus, I think," said Mike. "Not AP, though," he added. "What about another European history class, ya know like renaissance or something?"

"We gotta take Civics, with the Constitution and Declaration of Independence if we want to be ahead of the game," advised Wisner. "Our right winger, Mary Jane is taking that class."

"Well, G-d Damn, then we have to take it, don't we?" exclaimed Mike. "Ha, ha!"

"Let's do it," answered Wisner. "I mean it."

"Okay," replied Mike. "You talked me into it.

"Hmm, we have to take English again and some kind of science," muttered Wisner.

"Give me the English, but not the chemistry," declared Mike. "Maybe biology or ecological science."

"Biology's rough," said Wisner. "Take the ecological, or maybe geology?"

"Okay, Geology," said Mike. "What'a ya taking for gym class? I'm on the swim team."

"Study Hall," laughed Wisner. "What do you think of soccer team, or wrestling?"

"You can just take regular gym and side-step the pressure," shrugged Mike.

"Soccer will keep me in good shape," said Wisner.

"Okay, I'm going to make it official," said Mike, stepping up to the table with the lady and the computer.

※

While he and Mike were standing in line for classes, Wisner noticed Mary Jane Evans approaching. He smiled at her as she came up to him.

"I see you're still picking classes," she said. "I've already got all mine."

"Mike and I are taking Civics with you," he said.

"How did you do in the history class we had?" she asked.

"I got an A. I don't know what Mike got," he replied. "How did you do?"

"Well, he gave me a B. You know I came into the class real late," she replied.

"I got an A, too," interrupted Mike.

※

She was wearing raincoat and bluejeans, he could see. She even looked good with the rain hat on her head and rubber boots on her feet. Mike noticed that Wisner really lit up when the girl showed up.

"You're too good looking to be a hockey player?" said Mike, smiling at her.

"After I get spanked against the boards, I'm reminded," she laughed.

What did your dad say after he saw that happen?" asked Wisner.

"He was really shook up," she admitted. "But I'm okay. I'm going to finish the season."

"Watch out for those opponents. They may not even know you're a girl," said Wisner.

"But don't get into a brawl every time I get checked," she chided him.

"Yeah, I've got to watch out for that," he answered, glancing briefly at Mike.

◈

After signing up for his classes, Mike took leave of Wisner and Mary Jane and headed for the boys' gym. He walked up the steps and into the office and went quickly to where the swim team coach was sitting.

"Well, I'm signed up for the team, I just wanted you to know," he told the coach.

"Good to hear that Thomas," replied the coach. "Bring your goggles and trunks and stuff. We start practicing day after tomorrow."

"I'll be ready," Mike assured him.

"You still playing hockey?" asked the coach.

"Yeah, I've got a few more games," answered Mike. "I'll be finished before the league swim season starts."

"Well, don't get hurt," replied the coach. "We're going to need you."

◈

Mike walked out of the office and down the hall to the pool area. He went up to the door. It was locked so he looked in through the window. The pool was filled with water, tinted dark from the overcast outside showing through the side windowpanes. He stood there for several minutes thinking about the coming season. Swimming was a sport which involved individual performances with no teamwork required other than swimming skills and proper techniques. Relay races would be the only exception to that. With that in his thoughts, he made his way to the building exit and headed out of the school grounds. Tomorrow would be a full day attending classes. He would be walking home today. The snowfall had mostly subsided.

Chapter 12
Hockey Game for the Fans

Herb Wisner brought his mother, Wilma, and sister, Betty Lou, to the game. This was to be the last home game of the season and he wanted them to see what his chosen sport was all about. Until now, he had never tried to get them to see him play in the upper divisions. Before now, they had seen him play Pee Wee and possibly a Bantam game, which were probably boring to them. Playing Midget was another thing again. He escorted them to the bleacher seats and recommended they sit in the upper rows. He then hustled to the dressing room to finish suiting up. He found some of his teammates already there.

A few minutes later, Mary Jane came into the building, escorted by her dad. She was already dressed in her uniform except for the gloves. Her dad, Fred Evans, climbed up the home team bleachers and sat down alone. He waved to a few other hometown fans that he had seen there before. Mary Jane took off her skate guards and made her way to the home team bench and sat down with her two sticks and bag in hand. She looked tall in her skates, but obviously had a female look about her. She was five-foot eight in height and looked slender even in her shoulder pads.

Inside the dressing room, Bobby Rockford and Eric Johansen were chatting while wrapping some black tape on their stick blades. They got quiet when Wisner walked in. Sven Olavson was sitting quietly at another bench.

"Hi guys," called out Wisner.

"Hi yourself," called back Rockford.

After a few minutes, Wisner inquired, "Where's the coach?"

"Not here yet," replied Johansen.

Wisner pulled on his Bauer skates and tied the laces with a double knot. He carefully pulled off the guards and dropped them into his bag. He put on his elbow pads and pulled the hockey shirt over his head. His arms were visibly muscular. He had been working out with dumbbells at home and it was beginning to show results.

"Hey Wisner," remarked Bobby. "If I get checked into the boards, be sure and clobber the guy for me. But don't let the ref see it. We don't want you languishing in the penalty box while we're short handed."

"*Touché*," answered Wisner. "Point well taken and acknowledged."

Bobby looked at him for a second. "What's that mean, touché?"

"It means, I deserve the dig," explained Wisner. "I'm going to try to behave myself, this game. I screwed up last week. Anyway, it's a French word."

"Here, here!" yelled Bobby. "The man owns up!"

"Hey, listen," continued Wisner. "If anyone hurts Evans again, tackle me so I won't go bananas, okay."

"Well, yeah," chimed in Johansen, thoughtfully. "We gotta protect each other."

☙

Just then, Mike and Smith walked into the room.

"Rest easy, you guys," called out Smitty. "The stalwart defensemen are here!"

"Big deal, man," replied Bobby. "We were getting ready to forfeit the game, until you guys showed up. Now we can relax."

The teammates finished putting on their uniforms and sat waiting for the coach.

"How's swimming, Thomas?" asked Bobby. "You the big star again this season?"

"Pretty big, Rockford. But we sure could use you on the team," Mike answered.

"Yeah, right," answered Bobby.

ક

Minutes later, Coach Joshua came into the room.

"Good afternoon, fellas," he began. "This is our last home game. We have to win it for the hometown crowd, right?"

"Right!" howled the skaters.

"First of all," he continued. "These guys from Lynn Township are very disciplined. I talked to some of the other coaches. They pass a lot and score a lot of goals. They're going to pick on our weakest links. In our case, we've only got three defensemen so we're going to get tired. Try to relax out there when you're not puck handling or battling against the boards. Don't chase the puck as much on their side of the ice. Just stay in front of their puck handlers. Don't let 'em fake you out. Any comments or questions? No? Okay let's go."

ક

They filed out and sat down on the team bench. They were still making ice. Mary Jane sat there and looked at the other teammates. They nodded "Hello" to her.

When the Zamboni was done, the skaters made their entrance and went on with their warm up drills. Blakely was loosening up in front of the net, going through his blocking moves. The other team looked pretty good doing their warm ups. Finally the two officials, the ref and the linesman skated out and called for the face-off. Coach Joshua sent out the first line, Thomas, Smitty, Hurstmeyer, Rockford, and McAdoo. Mike skated out with Smitty, then whispered to him, "I'm gonna keep flipping the puck back to their zone and wear 'em down chasing the puck. That way maybe we have a chance to stay with these guys. Smitty looked at him and said, "Mike you're a genius!" Mike shrugged his shoulders.

The visitors got the puck on the face-off and began working it into the Laketown zone. Their defensemen kept passing the puck back and forth waiting for a good opening. Mike worked on muscling their wingmen and center away from the net. McAdoo finally stole the puck and passed back to Smitty. Smitty took it past the red line then flipped it to the visitor's zone, not far enough for an icing call. Eventually, the visitors worked the puck back to Laketown zone. After some fancy skating by the visiting center, the puck caromed back of the net where Mike dug it out and flipped it toward the other end of the rink. After three or four minutes, neither team had gotten off a good shot at the net. On the first line change, Mike stayed out with the second line. He scooted around a little when the puck went back to the visitors and went by Mary Jane and told her, "Play smart. Look for openings to get into position." She nodded in affirmation.

The visiting team worked the puck back to the Laketown zone and a defenseman took a hard shot at the net and Blakely blocked it smartly with the rebound going out to the front of the net. A battle for the puck ensued with it being eventually batted out to the right corner where Herb Wisner picked it up and skated behind the net to the other corner. He quickly changed directions and back to the right side where he passed to Sven Olavson. Olavson took it out to the red line where he was boxed in and lost it to an opponent winger who brought it back across the Laketown blue line and took a shot. It was blocked by the goalie and kicked over to Wisner who quickly took it out to center ice. He saw Evans waiting at the blue line and backhanded it to her. She crossed into the visitor zone, plowed forward, then passed it across to the fast moving, Wade Perkins, who flipped the puck by the defending goalie and into the net. The, the red light flashed again signaling a goal for the home team. The home town crowd was yelling their approval as Perkins, left winger on the 2nd line, skated across the ice to Mary Jane Evans with his stick held high. She got the assist. After a brief celebration, Coach Joshua changed lines for the face-off. He thanked the off going 2nd line as they made their way back to the bench. Perkins was getting high-fived by the others in his line. The score, home team ahead one nothing.

The puck was being carried back and forth down the ice throughout the rest of the first period. When the buzzer went off ending the period. Everyone headed back to the bench for a short respite. Before he sat down, Mike glanced up at the bleachers to see who was watching the game. He was surprised to see who was in the audience. It was the girl he had skated with that Friday night at the rink, Evelyn. "What was she doing here?" he thought. She was sitting with another girl from the high school. As he sat down, he scanned the rest of the crowd and recognized some of the regulars and parents of the players. His family was nowhere in sight.

"I don't know how you did it, team, but you held these guys scoreless, so far. Keep doing what you're doing," said the coach.

There was no response from skaters on the bench, since they didn't know what they were doing either, except for Mike and Smitty. They knew.

※

The 2nd line went out on the ice to start the second period. Smith and Wisner were the defensemen. Along with them were Olavson at center, and Perkins and Evans at wings. Lynn Township got the puck on the face-off and quickly brought it past the blue line. Perkins and Evans kept pressure on the Lynn defensemen who were looking for an opening. Eventually, the puck bounced off someone's stick and hopped over the boards and the ref called a time out. Mike, from his place on the bench, saw his father and mother climb up the bleachers behind him.

"Wow," he thought. "His mom was going to see him in action." It was late Saturday afternoon and they had apparently just closed up the yard for the weekend.

Coach took advantage of the timeout and called for a line change. Mike and the rest of his line skated out on the ice. On the ensuing face-off, Wisner who stayed out after the line change, got the puck, skated it out to center ice, and passed to Hurstmeyer. Before he could get it across the opponent blue line, it was taken away by the Lynn center, who took it quickly the other way. Mike tried to skate back and corral him but the puck was quickly passed to the opponent's left wing, who took it to the net, one on one with the goalie, and flipped it past Blakely into the net. The red light flashed, a goal for the visitors, the score now tied. A cheer went up from the visitor side followed by a groan from the hometown side. Things can change in a hurry with a breakaway happening like this. Mike went back to the net and gave Blakely a sympathetic pat on the helmet.

It was ten minutes into the period that saw both teams see-sawing up and down the rink with some excellent teamwork, but without a goal being scored. Both goalkeepers were doing a good job on the few shots that were tried. The two teams were playing a good defensive game shutting each other down. Mike was still flipping the puck to the opponent's zone and keeping them away from his net. On the next line change, Smitty and Wisner were at defense, with Olavson, Perkins and Evans up front. With Smitty and Wisner trading passes at the blue line, a visitor wingman was called for high sticking which left his team short handed. The Laketowners now had the advantage with the visitors being one man short. At one point, Wisner tried a slap shot, which didn't make it to the net but was quickly picked by Evans who flipped the puck back to Wisner. Wisner made a fake passing move to Smitty, then charged quickly towards the net and unloaded another slap shot that went past the goalie and into the net. The hometown crowd made a big roar of approval and it was 2 to 1, Laketown. Wisner skated in a big circle with his stick high in the air. It was only his second goal of the season.

The ensuing face-off found the visitors back at full strength and still struggling to get off a shot. The clock was ticking away the minutes. After another line change, the period came to an end. All the players skated back to their benches.

Said Coach Joshua to the team, "You're doing good you guys, but we gotta score more goals. They're only one shot away from a tie. You defensemen are doing a good job on their shooters but we may not be able to stave them off in the third period. So let's start skating more aggressively towards their side. They won't be expecting that. They think we're just being conservative. Evans, stay away from the boards and get closer to their net."

The Zamboni was back on the ice and the noise was drowning out the coach. The coach on the visitor's side was admonishing his team for not scoring any goals. He was telling his team to take more shots and not to wait for openings. Back on the Laketown bench, Mike looked up at his parents and then over to where Evelyn was sitting with her friend. She looked at him but didn't respond in any way. Moments later, the referee and linesman skated out on the ice as the Zamboni was making its exit.

The third period began with the Laketown first line back on the ice against the visitor's first line. The tempo was picking up with the visitors shooting from every angle once they came across the blue line. Mike got his stick on the puck from behind the net, skated out and flipped it back to the opponent's zone. The home teamers followed the puck except for Mike who stayed behind the line. This is the way Mike was playing most of the offensive situations. He didn't want the other team to get any breakaways. With the period half over, the game was getting a lot rougher with a lot of checking in the mix.

The visiting team came back later in the period and started pressing towards the net. After a few wild shots and saves by Blakely, the Lynn center backhanded the puck towards the net where it bounced off of Blakely's stick and into the net. The goal buzzer went off and it was now a tie game. Coach Joshua called a line change and the 2nd line took to the ice. Smitty stayed at defense with Wisner. After the visitor's scoring celebration, the ref dropped the puck on the face-off. The puck bounced out to Evans, who took it speedily to the other zone, turned and passed it back to Wisner following her at the blue line. She then skated in front of the visitor's net waiting for an opportunity. She was muscled off to the side by one of the defenders. The puck came in to her from the other winger and she took a quick shot without controlling it on her stick. It was blocked by the goalie, who then pushed it out to his left defenseman. The race was now on to the Laketown end of the rink. Wisner battled a winger for the puck and the ref blew his whistle for a standoff stoppage. From this point on, the battle continued with a lot of action but without another goal being scored. There were two minutes left in the period.

On the next stoppage, coach sent the first line back on the ice. On the face-off, the puck kicked out to Smitty on the right side and he took it out to center ice. He then paused from his journey and passed the puck to Mike over and back to the left. With a quick move, Mike faked left then took off right down the middle of the ice past one of the defenders. He leaned back, with his stick on the puck, to avoid a quick rush by the other defender, then faked right, then left, then shifted right again and flipped the puck into the net. The goalie was completely fooled by the maneuver. Mike quickly turned, skated back to the blue line, pumping his stick up and down over his head. The home team side of the bleachers howled out their approval. Mike's teammates then skated up and high-fived him.

The score was now 3 to 2, Laketown. After the face-off, the visitors tried feverishly to get off another shot but didn't get lucky. The home team kept flipping the puck back to the visitor end. Coach left the first line out on the ice during the last minute and a half. The buzzer sounded the end of the game with a logjam of skaters in front of the Laketown net. The home team bench emptied and the skaters congratulated each other on the victory. After the post game handshake rituals, the teams went back to their respective benches. Laketown coach walked across the ice to congratulate the other coach on a game well played.

Some of the fans came down from the bleachers to congratulate the team. Mike's mom and dad hugged him from behind. Mary Jane's dad came down to help her take off her shirt and pads. Even Herb Wisner's mother and sister came down to share their son's elation. "You looked good out there, brother," said his sister. Prior to going back to the dressing room, Wisner went over to Mary Jane and her dad and told her, "Nice going." He shook hands with her father, and said, "Thanks for coming," and then took leave. She had played a smart game and had very much contributed to the victory. When Mike stood up and huddled with his parents, he looked up to where the girl Evelyn was sitting. He saw that she was gone.

❧

After the dressing room activities, Ernie the rink manager came over to Mike walking out the door with his parents, and shook his hand.

"Nice going, Skates," he said. "You looked sharp out there. "See you Friday."

"Thanks Ernie," responded Mike.

"Is that what he calls you, Skates?" asked Mike's dad.

"That's me," admitted Mike.

Chapter 13
The School and the Pool

The school days were long and hard for Mike through the spring semester. After a rigorous day of solid subjects, it was down to the swimming pool for two hours of swim practice. First on the docket was 10 laps of freestyle warm up for everyone on the team. After a brief cool down, the team members moved along to their respective lanes to practice their specialties. Mike was feeling a little bit rusty after his long winter layoff. Playing hockey conditioned muscles for skating not swimming.

The school, being the only high school in the small town of Laketown, fielded a co-ed swim team. Mike greeted some of the returning swimmers from last season's team. The coach introduced the new recruits to the veterans. Mike was the one of two males scheduled for backstroke. Two girls were also signed up for it. There was some uncertainty about the breaststroke. Mike signed up for it, but so had three other people. The coach was going to have hold tryouts to make selections. Also, the team needed some good freestylers. This will also require some tryouts. The only thing Mike was assured of was his place on the backstroke events. He was by far the headliner in that style. On the second week of practice, Coach Allison held tryouts for free style. Mike came in third in the tryouts. Two males were ahead of him. The next school day, coach would hold tryouts for breaststroke.

The weather was starting to warm up a little in the Laketown area. The snowstorms had given way to the rains.

Mike had let his hair grow out during the winter, since he had not fallen prey to the white sidewall Fade craze. One afternoon, after some discussion with the swim coach, Mike made it over to the town barbershop. In the nuvo hi-tech school of thought, long hair slowed you down. When Mike walked into the shop with the slow turning barber pole, during a slow drizzle after swim practiced.

He stood at the doorway for a moment before sitting down. Two of the barber chairs sat empty. Mike noticed that the shop still had pictures of the traditional haircut styles. On the back wall was a photo of the barber holding up a large fish he had caught in some lake.

"Where you been, Michael?" asked the owner of the shop. "We thought you had moved away or something."

"I've been around," said Mike, grinning, after sitting down in one of the "wait your turn" chairs. Bill, the barber, had been the shop owner ever since before Michael was born.

In the first chair, Bill was working on a gray haired man with an old fashioned part in his hair. Mike recognized the man as the manager of the main street hardware store.

"Hi Mike," the man said.

"Likewise to you, sir," replied Mike.

Mike picked up a sports magazine and leafed through it. It was mostly an edition focused on major league baseball.

"I'm next, huh Bill?" asked Mike.

"That you be," answered Bill. "How's business at your dad's yard?"

"He's doing okay, I think. We're still in business."

"Well, when the weather improves, his business will pick up," said Bill.

"Yeah, I know," said Mike.

Bill stepped back, and handed his client the hand mirror to view the backside.

"That's the works, Frosty" said Bill, pulling off the cloth and brushing the man off

The man handed the mirror back to Bill.

"Looks okay, Bill. Thanks. Still 25 bucks?"

"Cash or credit card," replied Bill.

The man Frosty paid his bill in cash with a couple of singles for a tip.

The man put on his jacket and headed out the door.

"Next month, Bill?"

"Right," said Bill.

Mike got up and took off his jacket.

"Gimme a crew cut, Bill," said Mike. "It's swim season," he explained.

"Flat or round on top?" asked Bill.

"Round's okay," reassured Mike.

Mike settled back in the chair and Bill took out the clippers.

"I'm not shampooing your hair, Mike. It's too damn long and I'm cutting it all off."

"You're the guru here, Bill," said Mike. "Whatever you say."

"Your sister still away at school?" asked Bill.

"Yeah," replied Mike. "She's got a year and a half to go."

"You going to college, too?" asked Bill.

"Yes sirree," answered Mike. "That's a sure thing."

"Where to?" asked Bill.

"I'm not exactly sure," said Mike. "Maybe I can get a scholarship, probably some place in the state."

"Maybe for playing hockey, huh?" asked Bill.

"I get good grades, too," answered Mike.

❧

Mike showed up in school the next day looking like a stranger. There was no hair sticking out of his baseball cap. Bobby Rockford stared at him when he showed up in first period Geology class. He called out to Jake Hurstmeyer, sitting in the last row.

"Hey Jake, …. Jake, Mike's gonna need a smaller helmet for the next game. Maybe we can borrow one from the Pee Wees, ha, ha."

Mike just sat down, smiling and a little self-conscious. Some of the other students looked over at him. He opened his geology book and stared at a chart array of various fault lines. The teacher, Mrs. Stensgard, looked up from her desk to look at Mike.

"Hats off in the classroom, Michael," she told him. Then she stood up to start the lesson.

"We'll be studying minerals and rocks today, class. These are the basic building blocks on the planet. While I'm talking you can follow along in chapter 2 of the geology book you were given," she announced to the class.

Mike took off his hat and laid it on the floor under his chair. His hair was about a half inch long in most spots, a little longer on the top. He was fortunate enough to have a normal shaped head so there was nothing that embarrassing about it. He just looked a lot different to those who got used to his long hair. It was the school policy, not to allow students in school with shaved heads.

"The entire surface or crust of the earth is covered with rocks of some kind or another," droned on the teacher. "Some of it lies beneath a small layer of soil on land or sediment on the ocean floor. Mostly these rocks are an aggregate of inorganic chemical compounds. These compounds are known to us as minerals. There are three types of rocks, igneous, sedimentary, and the third class, metamorphic. Now be sure and take notes class as I am now going to show you the makeup of these rocks in a slide show on the projected screen on the front wall."

The teacher continued her lecture on the three categories pointing out major features with her mouse pointer on her computer screen. "Igneous rock being volcanic, sedimentary rock made up of clay, sand and gravel, and metamorphic, created by earthly pressures, heat, and solutions."

※

At the end of class, the teacher assigned a list of questions at the end of the chapter as homework. As the class filed out to the hallway, Jake, and Bobby waited for Mike to talk over his haircut.

"I did it for swimming, guys," he explained. "Long hair is a drag in the water and it slows you down in a race. How do I look? Not all that bad, I hope."

"Nah," said Jake. "Maybe the whole team ought to get crew cuts."

"Bad enough," laughed Bobby, who vowed to keep his hair long as a message for the rest of the world.

Next class was calculus on the floor above. Mike scooted straight up the stairs to the classroom since he already had his math book with him. He sat down hard in his chair, which was sitting right next to Wisner, who was also in the class.

"Hey, Mike, I didn't recognize you with the short hair. Let me guess. The swim coach told you to get it, right?" asked Wisner.

"You got all the answers, huh, Wisner," retorted Mike. "That's why I'm sitting next to you. Some of your brainpower will rub off on me."

"How'd you do in trig?" inquired Wisner.

"I got a B and I was lucky to get it," he answered. "I'm not all that good in math."

The class was taught by Mrs. McConnell, the same person that taught trigonometry. Mike knew some of the people from the trig class. Jennifer from chemistry was in the class. He felt that hanging out with her and Wisner would get him through the class. And maybe he would even learn the subject matter. It was all about domains, functions, relationships, integrals, and differentiations. He asked her if he could meet up with her at recess to go over any questions he might have. She told him okay, and he could always go to Wisner for help.

Mike forced himself to pay attention to the teacher's methodology and asked her a lot of questions. He started to realize that it was making sense to him. Wisner would nod to him whenever he was on the right track. Jennifer gave him the thumbs up after he voiced some of his solutions. Mike was feeling better about the class after the first couple of weeks.

∾

Third period, after recess, was American Literature. His English Lit teacher from the fall was the teacher for this class. He felt okay with this one, since he was a fast reader and remembered the important stuff. He liked the American writers as well or better than the English ones. Who woulda thought, Washington Irving, *The Legend of Sleepy Hollow,* Nathaniel Hawthorne, *The Scarlet Letter,* and John Steinbeck, the *Grapes of Wrath,* and who doesn't like Mark Twain. There'll be a lot of good reading this semester. And it should be noted that the one and only Evelyn Jurgenson was in the class. She still looked scary beautiful to Mike.

Fourth period was Spanish with the same teacher, Mrs. Spitzer, from the fall, and after lunch, it was Civics for fifth period. This was a tough schedule for Mike but he was determined to get into any college he chose. He hoped a couple of B's wouldn't hurt. Maybe he could study with Wisner or join some study group. Wisner would be the obvious choice for calculus and civics.

Swim team was working out well for Mike as he was getting his rhythm back. His backstroke was almost impeccable. He was still getting his breaststroke technique into a groove. He learned a lot just watching the girls practice. One afternoon just before the practice meets, Coach Allison approached him at poolside.

"Thomas, we might need you to double in the freestyle," he said. "I know you're working on your breaststroke but you gotta be practicing freestyle too. We got the relays and the medleys to worry about."

Mike looked intently at the coach before he responded.

"Whatever you say coach, if you think so."

"Yeah, one of our freestyle guys is having grade problems," he explained. "He might be put on probation. You'll have to swim in the freestyle heats."

"I'm a member of the team here coach," commented Mike. "I can swim freestyle. If you see any improvements I need, you have to tell me. I do freestyle with a stroke and a kick.

That's all I know. You'll have to give me any corrections with my form, I'm open for that."

"Okay, Thomas start practicing for it. I'll be watching," said the coach.

Mike walked over to another lane and dove in without a pause. He started stroking his arms and kicking his legs deliberately, not trying to go fast. He just wanted to build up his form. The turns would need practice too. His mind went blank to any extraneous thoughts. He just thought about his every move. He had to improve on his breathing rhythm. He had recently been practicing thinking about his physical moves, ice skating included.

⊷

Herb Wisner had decided to go out for the soccer team. He thought his hockey experience would help him fit in. He found dribbling the ball with his feet was a lot different from dribbling with a stick. He was already a senior so he was very late in mastering the sport. He was already entrenched into his class schedule so couldn't drop out of the team and switch to a gym class. That meant he had to stick with it. The coach had given him the position of a mid-fielder, which wouldn't require a lot of dribbling finess. He was comfortable with being on the team since it would keep him in good shape.

⊷

The soccer field was next door to the main athletic field where the track and field team practiced. The runners and field event people were practicing their events concurrently. The weather was mild, early in March, and the athletes were wearing their sweat clothes. Jogging around the track was a familiar face. Mary Jane Evans was trying out for a distance race. Being a senior, she was going to compete on the varsity.

The event she had chosen was the 800 meter run. The girl's track coach needed someone for the 400 meters and approached Evans about it a few days before. This was almost a sprint event so Evans hadn't made up her mind as yet. She wore a sweatband on her head to keep her hair up. Her stride was very easy and natural. She was obviously no stranger to long distance running. Somehow, she had the look of a top competitor. Her best time as a junior in the Milwaukee system was 2:35 minutes for the event. It looked like the Laketown hockey team wasn't going to take it easy after hockey season ends. Strangely enough, Mike thought that he was the only one on the hockey team going out for a school team.

Chapter 14
Friday Night Skating

Mike hurried home this Friday afternoon to get ready to go to his job at the rink. This would be a busy weekend for him. The hockey team was playing its last game of the season on Sunday afternoon. It would be an away game. He was somewhat relieved at an upcoming break from his busy schedule. The swim meets were to begin on the following Friday.

Mike's mother was at home fixing dinner for the family. When Mike got home he scrambled up the stairs to drop off his books. He came back downstairs with his jacket tossed over his shoulder.

"Hi, Mom," said Mike. "When is dad coming home? I need the truck to go to work tonight."

"He'll be home about six. If he's late you can take my van. I'm not going anywhere."

"Okay, thanks," he told his mother. "I have to get there by 6:15 to make ice for the first go round. When's dinner going to be ready?"

"Whenever you sit down, it'll be ready. It's spaghetti and meatballs. And here's a salad to start off with."

Mike sat down and started on his salad. After a few minutes, he said to his mom, "I've got a problem with my work load, Mom. What do you think of hiring somebody else for Saturday mornings to take my place? I've got a lot of schoolwork this semester. I've got five solid classes and the swim team."

"What about your Friday night job? Are you giving that up?"

"Nope, I like that one. I'm going to keep it. I need the money and I can practice my skating when I get the chance."

"Well," said his mother. "If we get someone for Saturday, we have to pay him more money than we pay you."

"Oh yeah," admitted Mike. He sat there thinking for a minute, then said, "What if I get one of my hockey teammates to replace me for maybe a few bucks more, like fifteen or sixteen bucks?"

"Who do think?" asked his mom.

"I'll talk to some guys Sunday at the game. I'll get someone," he offered.

"Well don't get us that Bobby Rockford kid," she exclaimed. "He's a little bit much for me!"

"Ha, ha!" laughed Mike. "Okay I'll get someone else."

∽

Mike drove the van over to the ice rink and parked in his usual spot, a distance from the rink. It was still dusk at this time of the year and not quite dark. When he came into the rink, he looked for Ernie in the office. Ernie was talking on the phone when he entered. Ernie put his hand over the phone and waved him out to the rink.

"Make ice," he told Mike.

Mike went out and headed over to the Zamboni room, but detoured to turn on the rink lights. He opened the garage door and then turned back to open up the side panels to the ice. He then went into the small garage and hopped aboard the Zamboni. He turned it on and backed out onto the ice, watching carefully over his shoulder. Once he entered the ice surface, he turned the machine around and made the rounds around and through the middle ice and smoothed out the surface. Every now and then, he hit the handle to lay more water. The sound of the Zamboni echoed through the building. All the while, Mike had enjoyed the chance to handle the Zamboni operation. When he finished the job, he turned the machine through the open panels and steered it into the garage. Once he was inside, he turned the key off, jumped down and closed the garage door behind him. He shoveled away the leftover ice scrapings and closed the panel doors. He looked across the rink to admire his handy work, and then walked briskly to the skate rental room to see what had to be done before the doors opened for the skaters. The doorman was standing near the entryway and was ready to go.

The doors opened at 6:45 and a few customers came in. Mike counted the money in his cash box and found the usual amount of change, $35. He heard Ernie in the next room sharpening some skates. He brought out his small pad of paper and laid it next to the register along with a small ballpoint.

Some groups were coming in to rent skates. Some of them were students from school who greeted him with a "Hi Mike" or a wave or sometimes both. Most of them were renting figure skates. A few of the skaters brought speed skates with them. They didn't stock them for renting at the rink. Hockey skates were usually brought in by hockey types, both younger guys and older. At about 7:30, Bobby Rockford came up to the window with his skates hanging over his shoulder.

"Mikey, I thought I'd do a few warm ups for Sunday's game," he said. "How do you like working here?"

"I'm glad to see you getting serious about sprucing up your footwork," said Mike. "Working here is a kick in the butt."

"Maybe I ought to get hired on here during the summer to supplement by life style needs," commented Bobby.

"You can ask the manager," replied Mike. "Maybe you can give skating lessons, like a class for hockey aspirants."

"How much do they pay you here?" asked Bobby.

"That's a military secret," chided Mike.

"Well, you handle the dough here, don't ya?" smiled Bobby.

"It ain't my dough," countered Mike. "And I ain't a thief, if that's what you mean?"

Bobby stood there for a minute, looked around at the rink, and said, "Well, I guess I'll put my skates on." He smiled and walked away.

After he left, Mike thought to himself, "I guess we've got at least one moron on the team."

The crowd was building up now and rentals were getting more frequent. At about 8:15, Evelyn Jurgenson came up to the counter.

"Hi, Evelyn," said Mike. "How's it going?"

"I heard you were working here," she said.

"How you doing in civics class?" asked Mike.

"I'm okay," she smiled. "I'll do okay."

"Same here," said Mike. "Need some skates?

"Yeah," she drawled. "Size twelve."

"Twelves? Not your size, is it?" quizzed Mike.

"For Johnny," she answered. "Not me."

"Just a minute," said Mike. "We've got 'em."

Mike walked back to the men's skate section and pulled out a pair that looked fairly new. He came back to the counter and set them down.

"Four bucks," he said.

She gave him a five and he opened the cash box, took out a one and put in the five and shut the drawer. Then he added a mark to his personal score pad.

"Thank you," he said, handing her the change.

She looked at him and asked, "What are you going to do after graduation? I see you're taking the advanced classes."

"I'm going to college," he answered. "Not sure which one. After that, maybe law school, maybe," he shrugged.

"I like your hair short," she smiled. "Later," she added. Then she turned and headed for the benches. Mike admired her gait as she walked away. "Hmmm," he thought. It was turning out to be an interesting night.

Ernie was playing some of his old favorites on the rink sound system. Must be from a CD or a tape. It didn't seem like it was radio. It was steady music with no interruptions.

Later that night, the returned rental skates were starting to pile up on the counter. Mike was busy trying to put them on the floor and out of the way. He had to make sure he tied the pairs together. The doorman came in to help him. Mike didn't want him anywhere near the cash box. He wasn't one to trust the human's basic urges.

At 11:00, they chased out the customers and locked the doors. Mike counted $327. Thirty-five of that was change money and $292 was for rentals. That was a big night. Seventy-three pairs rented out. He checked his check off pad. Seventy-two pairs. Once again he forgot to make one mark. He reported his count to Ernie, who put the cash into a bank bag.

"Here's your money, Skates" he said to Mike. "Twenty-five bucks, okay?"

"Okay with me," said Mike. "See you next week."

☙

Mike put on his baseball cap and jacket and headed out to the parking lot. There was still some activity with customers milling around. Mike got into the van and drove home. He remembered he still had to work the next day so he had to get to bed.

Chapter 15
Game at Atkinson Creek

Bill Thomas was doing sixty down this two-lane road leading to Atkinson Creek. In the pickup truck with him were his son Mike and Donny Smith. Hockey bags and sticks had been tossed back into the truck bed. It was early Sunday morning in late March and traffic was light.

"It looks like we left home before the rest of the people woke up and decided to go somewhere," noted Mike.

"Yeah, Mike, it's a little early, but you never know about traffic," said his dad. "I don't like you to be late for a game."

"Yeah," injected Donny. "And this is the last game of the season. Too bad we didn't qualify for the playoffs."

"And the last game in the youth program for us high school seniors," continued Mike. Are we ever going to play another hockey game? Well maybe in college. Most of the schools have teams or hockey clubs."

"Most of you guys will want to keep playing somehow or other," said Mike's dad.

"Oh, I'll keep on playing," said Donny.

"Me too," said Mike.

∽

Bill Thomas turned the truck on to a road that was named Creek Road and eventually across a short bridge over a narrow river. They noted the river was running high from the melting snow in the nearby hills. A short distance away they came upon the main street of a big town. The approaching sign read, "You are now entering Atkinson Creek city limits -

Population 3,250 – Elevation 110 feet." They kept driving slowly past the many stores and buildings until the reached a large building housing an ice rink. They pulled into a driveway and parked in the rink's parking lot. There were about six cars in the lot and a small RV.

The boys piled out of the pickup and pulled their hockey gear out of the truck bed. Mike's dad locked up the truck and put on his jacket and followed the boys to the rink entrance. They all entered together and looked around the rink. They had been there before so everything looked the same. The boys were dressed in their street clothes so they would have to go to the dressing room to change. Mike's dad sat down on a bleacher plank and opened a magazine.

Mike and Donny Smith found the visitor's room empty. They were the early birds. It was 9:15 AM. The game was scheduled for 10:00 or shortly thereafter. They slowly changed into their pads and uniforms.

"I wonder if Evans is gonna show?" commented Donny. "She's on the track team now."

"Oh really," responded Mike, with a surprised look. "Surprise, surprise!"

Just then, the door opened and Wisner, Jake, and Bobby came in talking loudly.

"Is this it?" exclaimed Bobby. "Is this all we got?"

"Blakely and McAdoo are coming with the coach," replied Jake. "We're covered!"

"Hurry up and get changed, Bobby," said Donny. "You know I have to tie your skates for you."

The rest of the boys laughed. After a short while, Perkins and Olavson came in.

"Coach just pulled up with a couple of guys," said Perkins.

"What about the home team? Are they here yet," asked Bobby.

"They'll be here, don't worry," said Mike.

※

All the Laketown players had arrived by the time the ice was ready. The home team starters were taking their places for the face-off. Coach Steenberg sent out the first line to set the tone of the game. The home team wore jerseys that resembled those of the New York Rangers. The opposing centers wore the big "C" on their jerseys to denote them as team captains. The ref dropped the puck and the game was on. After bouncing around near the sideboards, the puck was picked up by the home team and passed back to one of the defensemen. They worked it up past the red line where it was stolen by Rockford, who tried to get it past the opponents blue line. He worked it into the left corner where he was tied up by the opposing center. After some stick poking and kicking it slid out to Mike who circled around with it then passed it out to Smitty on the right. Smitty flicked it to McAdoo in the direction of the net. McAdoo never got it as it was intercepted by the opponent's center, who quickly skated it out to middle ice. Mike noted that the other center was quick on his skates. He hurried to cut him off before getting a breakaway. He slowed him down enough to give Smitty a chance to get back in position. Now the puck was in the visitor's zone. The Atkinson defensemen were working it around and passing it back and forth looking for an opening. After a while, one of them took a slap shot, which went wide left and was chased down by Mike who moved it to middle ice. He passed it to McAdoo on the right who took it across the blue line into enemy territory. At this point, Laketown sent in Olavson at center and Wisner to replace Mike. Eventually, Perkins and Evans came in to replace the wingers. The game was three minutes into the period.

The puck was now working its way back and forth by the two teams. Perkins tried a backhand shot which was blocked nicely by the opponent's goalie. The puck came out to Evans who passed it to Smitty. Smitty tried a slap shot, which never reached the net, bouncing off someone's stick and into the opponent's corner. At this point, both teams changed lines and Mike was back on the ice with Wisner. It was five and a half minutes into the period. The home team now controlled the puck and skated it into the visitor's zone. A shot by the opponent's center missed the net and went into the corner, where Wisner picked it up, skated behind the net to the left side and passed it up to Jake. Jake skated it across the blue line and side flicked it to Rockford. Rockford hit it hard towards the net where McAdoo skated with it in a circle and took a forehand shot. The goalie shot his stick out, but not fast enough and the puck hit the net. The ref signaled goal and McAdoo skated away from the net with his stick in the air. The score was now one nothing, visitors.

Coach Joshua stood up from the bench and clapped his hands together in celebration. The first line stayed in for the face-off. The loose puck was picked up by Mike, who promptly flipped it into the Atkinson zone, and the chase was on to retrieve it. With that, Smitty skated out to relieve Wisner at defense. By the end of the period, the score stood visitor's one, home team zero. When everyone was seated on the bench, Coach Joshua told the guys to take a lot of shots since this was the last game and they had nothing to be conservative about.

Mike looked around to see who had come down to watch the game. He saw his dad, Mary Jane Evans' mom and dad, and Jake Hurstmeyer's mom and dad. He stretched a little and saw Perkin's mom sitting with another woman. That was it except for a few strangers, from hereabouts. The opposition supporters sat on the same side since there was only one side of the rink with bleachers. After a few minutes, the teams came out for the second period. The second line, Olavson and company, would do the face-off. Smitty came in at defense with Wisner.

During the first two minutes, the home team was mostly in control of the puck. Eventually, one of their wingers popped one into the net, over Blakely's shoulder and the score went to one-one. The hometown fans let out a big whoop at this bit of good fortune. Laketown coach sent out the first line to settle things down on the ice. Wisner came out and Mike went in.

Mike glided up to Smitty and said quietly, "Let's flip the puck to the opponent's side, like we did that time before. We'll see what happens."

Smitty nodded in agreement. The ref dropped the puck for the face-off and the action began. The home team got the puck and brought it across the blue line. The Laketown wingers went after the puck handlers. There was a lot of banging it around and when Mike or Smitty got it they flicked it over the red line and beyond and took chase. The opponents had to chase it back in their own end. Whenever the visitor's got control at the enemy blue line, Mike and Smitty flipped it toward the net. This gave the winger's and center more shots on goal. On the next line change, Mike told Wisner the same thing. On one exchange, Evans got control of the puck and took a shot from the right side of the rink, and a few seconds afterwards, she got checked hard by an enemy winger, knocking her backwards into the boards. On the next whistle, Mike skated by the Atkinson center and said, "I don't like the way your guy checked my winger. She's running track this season. We don't want her getting hurt."

"Hey dude," replied the center. "My guy is a girl, too!"

At that, Mike skated back and tapped his blade on the ice.

"Huh," he said to himself. "Imagine that."

It was eleven minutes into the period with the score still tied. Mike was still playing it conservatively, flipping the puck to the other zone. Coach Joshua was aware of the strategy. He would let it go on for a while.

As the period went on, things got a little rougher. Winger Perkins got two minutes in the penalty box for roughing. The visitors were now shorthanded. Olavson was the only skater chasing the puck. After a minute and a half into the penalty, Mike got the puck, made a motion to ice it, then pulled back his stick and took off on the right side with the puck, ducking in and out on the way. On a slight pause, he saw Olavson cutting alongside him on his left, then passed it to him. Olavson took a quick slap shot by the goalie and into the net. The red light went on for a score. Olavson was hugged by Mike and raised his stick in the air. The visitors were back in front, two to one. Coach changed the line with three replacements only since it was a shorthanded goal. There was still thirty seconds to go, shorthanded.

The period ended without another goal and Laketown ahead. The coach put his foot up on the bench and said to the team, "We can play it close to the vest or we can go wild. It we play it close, they can still catch us. If we go wild, anything can happen. This is our last period. Just don't get careless. Stay focused."

"Way to go, Laketown!" somebody called down from the stands.

Mike took a drink of water out of his bottle and walked over to Mary Jane.

"You okay," he asked.

"Un huh," she answered, with a smile. "I'm okay."

"That guy that checked you is a girl too," he said. "Be careful of the boards."

∽

The Zamboni had just finished making ice and was now leaving. The second line started the third period. Smitty was out on the ice with Wisner. The game was getting a little more intense. Since the score was close, Atkinson knew they could still win it. Their wingers were coming after the Laketown defensemen in the corners. Wisner and Smitty were fighting hard to control the puck. Whenever he could, Smitty would send the puck to the other end. Sometimes it would get an icing call. Wisner was doing the same. Finally after what seemed an eternity, the first line went back out on the ice. Wisner stayed on the ice this shift. Smitty came off. Next time the visitors got the puck, they passed back to the defensemen to set up the strategy. Mike wanted to keep the puck away from his net. He motioned to Smitty to stay back with Blakely. The strategy to keep the puck away seemed to help out.

During a timeout when the puck was knocked outside the ice area, Mike suggested that the center play the blue line in place of the right defenseman and leave the wings to play the net. This left the one defenseman back to protect the goalie from a breakaway situation. The coach nodded okay to that.

Thinking to himself, the coach wondered at the extreme planning that was taking place for the last non-critical game of the season. There was about ten minutes left to go in the game. This showed a lot of character on the part of the team.

On the other side of the ice, the Atkinson coach was instructing his team on the ensuing game plan.

"Their defensemen are making us work harder by flipping the puck back to our zone and making us skate it out again. We're going to have to come back fast. I'm going to change lines a lot to keep us fresh. We've got twelve skaters. They only have nine. They only have three defensemen. They're going to be tired before the game is over. You wingers crowd the crease so we can keep their goalie busy. Got it?"

They answered in the affirmative.

The game got underway with Laketown controlling the puck. It was the line with Wisner, Mike, Perkins, Olavson, and Evans. At the blue line, Mike flipped the puck into the right corner. Olavson and an opposing defenseman spent several seconds fighting over it. The opponent finally flipped it around the back of the net where it was picked up by the other defenseman. He was met by Perkins who deflected it to an opponent winger who started moving it up the ice towards the visitor zone. Wisner and Mike backed up in a hurry to protect Blakely. The puck changed hands during this go-round without any shots on goal. The minutes were ticking away. Coach Joshua changed lines with Rockford, Hurstmeyer, McAdoo, Smitty, and Mike staying on this line. The Atkinson team was sending in replacements on a frequent basis.

With five minutes left, the Atkinson team was controlling the puck in the Laketown zone. The defensemen were trading passes looking for someone in front of the net. The left defenseman suddenly pulled the trigger with a quick slap shot, which was blocked by Blakely with a dramatic stick maneuver. The puck bounced to his right just outside the crease and was poked into the net on the rebound by an Atkinson winger. The referee signaled goal and the red light went on. The hometown fans raised an emotional outcry in celebration. The score was now tied two to two. The visitors were stunned by the sudden turn of events. Mike bent down with his hands on his knees breathing hard. The teams skated around in preparation for the face-off.

The strategy was changed with this turn of events. Both teams would have to go on the offensive. The Laketown team could no longer play conservatively. They had to go for the goal. Wisner skated out on the ice and relieved Mike. Mike noticed Evans was still on the bench, not going out with her line. It was getting very rough out on the ice with the increasing intensity of the game. Everyone was checking everyone else on the opposing teams. The face-off went to the home team who brought the puck across the visitor blue line. Winger Perkins battled an opposition winger for the puck. It ended up behind the visitor net where Smitty skated it around from side to side. Eventually he passed it to Wisner, who skated it up through center ice. There was three minutes left. Wisner skated it up and passed it to Olavson, who tried to force it through to the net. Eventually, the puck was back to Wisner who spun around trying to find and opening. As he turned around an opponent's stick banged against his right forearm. Afterwards the puck ended up on the other side where Smitty picked it up and sent it down to the enemy corner. Wisner skated towards the visitor bench holding his right arm with his left. Mike quickly headed out to the ice to relieve him. Wisner sat down on the bench with his head down.

They were now in the last minute of the game. The home team had the puck. One shot was blocked by Blakely and bounced away. The home teamers still controlled the puck. Another shot on goal that defenseman Perkins deflected out to another hometown skater. Another shot and the puck hit the left bar and rolled back to a defenseman. The defenseman passed to the center, who whacked it hard past Blakely and into the net. The ref signaled goal and the home team celebrated wildly with sticks in the air. There was ten seconds left on the clock.

The ensuing face-off was mostly a formality with the short time left in the period. Mike got the puck in the melee and sent a long slap shot wide of the opponents net. The buzzer went off signaling the end of the game. The hometown fans were applauding their team's comeback. The teams went back to opposite sides of the rink to start the high-five ritual. The coaches shook hands in the middle of the ice. The teams went back to their benches and sat down momentarily.

※

"Nice going you guys," exclaimed the coach to his team. "You played a damn good game. Don't fret over the score."

Mike went over to Wisner who was talking to Mary Jane seated on the bench next to him. They both had their helmets off.

"What happened Wiz?" asked Mike. "You okay?"

"No Mike. I think my wrist is busted or something in my forearm."

"Oh Christ!" Mike cursed. "You got hurt in the last game. Shit!"

"Yeah," muttered Wisner. Ain't that the shits!"

Mike looked at Mary Jane. She had tears in her eyes.

"You aren't hurt, too, I hope?" he inquired.

"No, I'm fine," she answered. "Coach kept me out of the game when it was getting too rough at the end."

"Who'd you come with, Wiz?" asked Mike.

"I came with Jake," he replied.

"We gotta get you checked out at an ER somewhere," exclaimed Mike.

"We're going to take him back," said Mary Jane. "We'll take him to an ER."

⁂

Mike thought for a moment then said, "You better call home and have your mom or dad meet you there. You're still under aged. You need their consent and insurance and stuff. You're not eighteen yet, are you?"

"No, not yet," said Wisner.

"You know where to take him back home?" he asked Mary Jane. "The hospital in town has an ER section. Take him there."

⁂

Mike trudged back to the dressing room. He felt like getting out of his hockey clothes. A few of the guys were still there. McAdoo and Blakely were there, getting dressed. They had come with the coach.

"Nice going you guys," called out Mike. "We came damn close to winning."

"Thanks, Mike," responded Blakely. "Likewise to you."

"Hey, Blake," called Mike. "You working at all, part time, I mean?"

"Yeah, I work down at the drug store on Sundays, usually" he replied.

"What about you, Mac? You working?"

"No, not at the moment," he replied.

"You want a job on Saturday mornings, at my dad's lumber yard?" asked Mike. "The pay ain't great, but it's okay," he added.

"Yeah, sure," he replied. "Don't you work there?"

"No, I work at the ice rink on Friday nights. I don't wanta work on Saturday. I've got too much homework," he explained. "Are we set then?"

"Yeah, we're set. When do I start?"

"Next Saturday," replied Mike.

❦

Mike got changed in a hurry, wiping himself off with the towel in his hockey bag. He hurried out of the room and looked for his dad and Smitty. They were sitting in the bleachers waiting.

"Let's go, Dad. I'm ready."

They made their way out of the rink and into the bright sunlight. It was still kind of chilly. They threw their bags and sticks into the truck bed and got into the cab.

"You guys were awesome," said Mike's dad. "I'm pretty damned impressed."

"Thanks, Dad," said Mike.

"Thanks, Mister Thomas," said Donny.

"Uh, Dad," I got a guy to work the yard on Saturdays. It's McAdoo, our winger. He's a good guy. He needs the dough."

"Well, I'm not going to make him rich," joked his dad.

"No, we gotta make you rich, Dad," laughed Mike.

∽

They were mostly quiet on the ride back to Laketown. It was kind of a long ride. There wasn't a lot of scenery to look at, just some farms and some low rising hills. Mike and Donny talked a little about their classes at the high school. When they reached Laketown, Mike told his dad to drive them to the hospital. He wanted to check on Wisner. The hospital was located a half mile this side of the lumberyard. They pulled into the parking lot. There were four other cars parked there.

Hey Dad, Smitty and I will go in," he said. "You can watch our bags in the back, okay. We won't be long. C'mon Smitty."

They went into the ER doorway and were greeted by a guy behind a counter.

"We have a buddy, who just came in, I think, with a girl," he explained. "With an arm injury."

"Just a minute," the guy said. He picked up a phone and spoke to somebody about it.

"Yeah go on in," said the guy. "He's here."

They walked into the waiting room and Mary Jane's parents were sitting there. They looked up and said, "Hi."

"Oh, he's inside already, huh?" asked Mike.

Fred Evans, Mary Jane's father, replied, "Yes he's inside now. They'll x-ray him. My daughter is inside, too, and so is his dad.

Mike and Smitty sat down.

"Tough luck," said Donny Smith. "Getting hurt in the last game."

"You kids play a tough sport," acknowledged Fred Evans.

"Your daughter is pretty tough, too," exclaimed Mike. "She must be a standout in the girl's league, I bet."

"She's good," said her dad.

Mike and Smitty sat for a while. After about ten minutes, Mike got up and said, "We have to leave. My dad is waiting out in the truck for us. Please tell Wisner we were here. Thanks. And thanks for coming to the game, folks."

The Evans nodded and waved goodbye as the two boys departed.

Chapter 16
Swim Meet

The Laketown High swimming pool was all lit up for the afternoon event. There was a scattering of early arrivals in the stands. It was 2:30 PM and the meet with Braunsville High was scheduled for 3:30 PM. School was just letting out for the day. Team members were inside the gym next door putting on their swimsuits. The visiting team bus had just pulled up and was unloading team swimmers and their coaches. The visiting team filed into the pool building and sat down on the team benches. The Laketown swimmers were starting to come into the building from the gym area. The home team colors were gray and orange. The visitors wore blue sweats with yellow trim letters.

  The rival swim coaches waited for their team to settle in before giving last minute instructions. The swimmers were already schooled as to their swim styles and needed very little in that regard. Strategies might be changed in some cases. When the meetings were over, the swimmers stripped down to their trunks and tried out the water, with the visitors taking the left lanes and the home team, the right lanes. Mike Thomas took turns practicing his freestyle and backstroke. On the backstroke he concentrated on his starts. He looked ready for both events. The medley relay would start it off. He would be doing the backstroke leg. His next race afterwards would be the 50 meter freestyle. His backstroke race would come near the end. He was also scheduled for one leg of the 400 meter freestyle relay.

The swimmers were going through their stretching routines to loosen up. Mike needed this more than most others with all his tense hockey conditioning. He would be first in the water for his backstroke leadoff in the medley. He put on his swim cap and goggles then stretched his hands down to his toes.

The swimmers were alerted to enter the water. Once in the water they grabbed the handlebars on the wall and planted their feet. Mike paid no attention to the crowd of students entering the indoor pool stadium. In a few seconds, the starters were all in position. At the sound of the loud beep, Mike vaulted backwards into his dolphin maneuver. He started his kick and then his first backward arm stroke. He was in one of the middle lanes feeling all alone. Three other racers hit the water around him. Mike felt a little tight at first but then got into his groove and racing rhythm. He stayed this rhythm all through his leg. He knew he had mastered the form of this event so just kept doing what he was doing. The crowd was shouting its encouragement as the swimmers neared the opposite end. In a short while, Mike felt his hand hit the wall and saw the breaststroker diving over him into the choppy water.

"C'mon out, Mike. Give me your hand," said the anchor swimmer above him.

Mike pulled himself out of the water and walked to the back wall to shake off. He turned around to watch the action. The butterfly members of the relay teams were leaning forward on the platform blocks ready to dive in. He saw the guy in his lane dive off first. Good – his team had the lead. The freestyle anchorman in his lane was their fastest swimmer. He climbed up on the blocks and set himself. The other anchors did the same. The butterfly swimmers conveyed a different look to the sport, bouncing in and out of the water coming towards him. After a minute, the anchormen dove into the water and it was now or never. Mike thought that his freestyler dove in first. That was a good sign.

The crowd in the bleachers was shouting, "Go, go, go!"

Mike started walking to the other end of the pool to meet up with the rest of the relay team. He was followed closely by the butterfly swimmer. It looked like his guy was ahead. It was over before he got there. His fellow teammates were raising their hands to celebrate the team's victory in the first event. The hometown crowd was up and cheering in the bleachers. Mike hugged the other relay swimmers then found a seat on the bench. He turned around and grabbed a white towel out of the towel bin and wiped off.

It was the girl's turn to do the medley, but Mike had to get ready for his part in the 50 meter freestyle race a little later.

He turned to one of the relay guys and asked, "How did I do in my leg?"

"You won, Mike," was the answer. "Good job, dude!"

∽

The girls came out losing their medley, but not by much. It was close and the coach was glad. The next race was the boy's 200 meter freestyle. Mike wasn't in that one. Two boys from each team were in it.

The race began and the crowd noise scaled up during the race. It looked like another winner for the home school. It looked like coach was going to have a good freestyle team. The race ended with a first and second place victory for Laketown High.

∽

Sitting up in the bleachers and giving vocal support were Bobby and Jake from the hockey team. Absent were Wisner and Evans, among his close friends. They were both on varsity teams so didn't expect to show, anyway. Mike's mom and dad were both at work and couldn't be there. His dad had never come to one of his swim meets in all the years he had competed. His mom had come to a few.

∽

Laketown had edged out Braunsville in the Individual Medley Relay and were now ahead in the team scoring. It was now time for the 50-meter freestyle race. Each team had three entrees. Mike was in lane seven, on the outside. He took off his light jacket and pants and put on his goggles and cap. He climbed up on the starting blocks. Some of the swimmers had shaved off their chest hair, but Mike didn't believe in that so there appeared quite a contrast of bodies on the starting line. They all leaned forward in the ready position.

At the sound of the beep, they dove forward like missiles into the pool. Mike did his dolphin up and down movement after he hit the water, and then started stroking. The crowd let out a roar of encouragement to their favorites. It was a short race so Mike was kicking hard. It was the strongest part of his swim technique. He was reaching farther and farther with his arms. Moments later he touched the opposite wall, his race over. The crowd noise was subsiding as all the contestants finished. Mike looked over at the scoreboard and saw his number. He had come in third. He was in the money. His fastest teammate and an opponent had come in ahead of him. He wasn't going to complain about that. His time was right up there. He high-fived his teammates and then climbed out of the pool. The coach shook his hand as he dried off. The relay time was 1:30.04

"Yaa, Mike," he heard someone call out from the bleachers. He had some fans in the audience. He raised his right hand in response.

The following events went by in a haze for him. They were starting and ending so quickly, he couldn't keep up. In a half hour later, he would be swimming in another event, the first leg in the 200 meter freestyle relay. And right after that, the 100 meter backstroke. This wasn't the best planning for his part in the meet. But he was just a beginner in the freestyle events so the coach was starting him in the short 50 meter races.

His breathing was back to normal when the time for the next relay arrived. He took off his light jacket and pants and did some stretching. He put on his goggles and swim cap and huddled up with the other relay participants. He was first in the blocks. There was only the Braunsville relay team opposing them. Laketown had lane 3 and Braunsville, lane 5. Mike climbed up on the starting block platform. His relay contact was ready on the opposite side of the pool. Both sides were in place when the beep sounded. Mike had to remember his breathing pattern. When he hit the water and wiggled his way to the surface, he was kicking hard and stroking in concert. He had to concentrate on his technique, which is what he had psyched himself into doing. He stayed with his game plan and was making good progress. He wasn't thinking about anything else. Once in a while he wondered what the hell he was doing in the water. At the other wall, he touched it in good fashion and stayed low as the next man dove over him. He quickly got out of the water and stepped around the anchorman who would finish the race. He walked around to the other side watching the swimmers. It was close, with his teammates slightly ahead. It would be up to the anchorman to bring home the gold medal. He felt that he did pretty well in his leg to keep them in the race.

He grabbed a towel and tried to relax. His part in the backstroke would be coming up soon. He watched as his teammate touched the wall first to score a victory in the relay. He high-fived the other relay swimmers, and then sat down. Next would be the girl's freestyle relay. Some of the girls on the team were new to the varsity and were untried in a meet. None of the girls on the team were members of any pseudo elitist group, which was good for the team.

The school band was in attendance and struck up some inspirational songs, which was good for Mike because it would push back the time of his next race. Afterwards, the girls lined up for their relay race. The sound of the beeper going off kicked off the vision of the two girls on the blocks diving off in synchronization and knifing into the water at the same time. The crowd in the bleachers came alive with the cries of encouragement. It was a good race. The Lakewood team was ahead until the last leg when the Braunsville girl pulled ahead at the end.

※

It was now the big moment for Mike Thomas. The backstroke was his specialty and he was expected to win. He had won the backstroke leg of the relay to start things off. He stood next to the pool with his cap and goggles on. He eased himself down into the water in lane 2. He was racing against one teammate and two rival swimmers. When all were in there proper positions, the beeper to start sounded. Mike took off backwards wiggled into position and started kicking and stroking. "Stay synchronized," he thought to himself. He was reaching backward and kicking hard. "Stay with it," he told himself, as he kept churning. After a time he was reaching the point near the opposite wall to turn for the return leg. On his turn he drifted a little to one side, but righted himself to catapult off the wall. He was back on his rhythm again and headed for the finish line. After another minute, he touched the wall and his race was over. He came up and turned to the scoreboard and saw he had finished first. He raised his right hand in celebration.

"Way to go, Mike!" came a call from the bleachers, amidst the cheering.

"I'm guessing that was Rockford," he thought to himself. He took off his goggles and climbed out of the pool. Somebody handed him a clean towel and he wiped himself down. He looked at his time. It was 52 seconds. Not that great. He sat down to watch the girls back strokers. A few minutes later, Coach Allison walked up to him and said, quietly, "The judges disqualified you, Mike. Sorry. They say you strayed out of your lane on the comeback turn around. What happened?"

"I was afraid of that, coach," he replied. "When I was setting myself to push off, I got off the mark. I didn't think I strayed out of my lane though."

"Well, the judges say you did," said the coach.

The beep sounded for the girl's race. The coach turned and walked away. That was the last race for Mike. He did two individual races and two relays. Well, at least he helped win the relays. Mike hung around for the last two races. He was interested in watching the breaststroke heat. The home team lost that one, but they won the 400 meter freestyle relay to top it off. On the team scorecard, Laketown boys were victorious. The girls were not that close in a losing effort.

After the last race, Bobby and Jake came down from the bleachers to talk to Mike.

"Hey man, what happened in your backstroke?" inquired Bobby. "You finished 10 feet ahead of the next guy!"

"I got disqualified by making a bad turn at the other end. I don't know how that happened," answered Mike. "I'm working on a string of bad luck here. We lost our last hockey game and now I screw up in a swim meet. Well the team won, anyway."

"You did good in the relays, Mike," consoled Jake. "You're looking good for a hockey player in a pool."

"I gotta get dressed," said Mike, excusing himself. "I've got a lot of homework. See you guys. Thanks for coming out."

After changing into his street clothes, Mike went home on his mountain bike, a little disappointed in his backstroke screw up.

Chapter 17
Friday Night Skating

It was still light when Mike reached the ice rink. He had the pickup truck this night. It was only 5:30 so he decided to do a little skating on his own before the rink opened for business. He knocked on the door until Ernie unlocked and opened it. He saw Mike had his skates and a stick with him.

"Hey, Skates, you're early," he said.

"Hi Ernie," he replied. "I'm going to get in a little practice before we open. Then I'll make ice."

"Okay, Skates, have at it."

Mike went over to the customer benches and changed into his hockey skates. He glided out on the ice doing figure eights, forward and backward, then practiced his quick stops. He followed up, dropping a puck and pushing it forward with stick handling movements up and down the ice. He took a few flip shots against the boards during the process. Finally, he did a few wind sprints down the middle of the rink. He then went back to the benches and changed back to his street shoes. It was 5:55 PM. He put his skates and stick on top of a shelf in the rental room.

He opened the Zamboni garage, opened up two panels, and then backed out and drove around the inside of the rink to start the ice making process. By now he was getting good at it. He made himself pay attention to what he was doing. That way he avoided screwing up. He did a good job as usual. After parking the Zamboni, he headed toward the office to check in with Ernie.

"What's new, Ernie?" he asked.

"I'm going to teach you how to sharpen skates. I can't get bogged down with that every day."

"If you can wait until school's out in a few weeks I can work more hours," said Mike.

"I'll teach you now, so you'll be able to take over when I get too busy. I do about ten a day. That's about all I can handle. Stick around after closing and I'll check you out on it. Maybe for about a half-hour."

"Okay, Ernie," agreed Mike. "Now I'm going to learn the whole rink business," thought Mike to himself.

∽

In the rental room, Mike checked the money drawer. There was the thirty-five bucks. The skates were all in their bins, he noted. He sat down on his chair and pulled an ROTC manual out of his jacket pocket. He looked it over for a few minutes until the rink opened. He had to find out what colleges had the ROTC program.

It didn't look like they were going to have a big crowd tonight, not with the final exams coming up soon. Some families were coming in with their younger kids. It might turn out to be a little kid night. He dealt out about seven pairs of the smaller sized skates in the first 20 minutes. About 7:30, Herb Wisner came in with his favorite female, Mary Jane Evans. They came over to the rental counter to see Mike. Wisner was still wearing his cast.

"What are you guys doing here tonight?" exclaimed Mike. "You should be home studying. You're not going to put on skates are you, not with Mary Jane running track?"

"Nope," replied Wisner. "We're going to a movie. Just for the hell of it. I need a break."

"Did you pay to get in?" asked Mike.

"No. I told the guy at the door we were just watching," said Wisner.

"Wait a second," said Mike, walking away to wait on a customer.

When he came back, Mary Jane asked him if he liked working there.

"It's the best job I ever had," he joked. "I'm learning the business."

"Have you figured out where you're going to college?" asked Mary Jane.

"No, but I'm close to deciding," answered Mike. "How about you two? Have you applied yet?"

"Yeah, we want to go to the same school, it turns out," said Wisner.

"No kidding," laughed Mike.

"We're going to take off, Mike," stated Wisner. "We'll let you get back to work."

Mike nodded and waved goodbye.

※

At about 10:00 PM, a couple of guys came in and approached the counter. They weren't looking too steady on their feet.

"We need some skates," one of them said. He was about 6 foot one and was wearing a sport jacket.

"What size?" asked Mike.

"I'll take a size 12 and my buddy, a size 10 ½."

"We got mostly full sizes, not half sizes," explained Mike. "I'll give him an eleven."

"Okay, okay," said the big guy.

Mike brought up the skates.

"Eight bucks," he said. "Four bucks for each pair."

"That's too much," the guy said.

"That's the price," said Mike.

The guy handed Mike a ten spot. Mike gave him two dollars change.

"Didn't I give you a twenty?" the guy asked.

"Not a chance," said Mike, holding up the ten dollar bill. "See?"

"Oh, okay," said the big guy.

"Are you guys okay to skate?" asked Mike. "Do you know how?"

"Sure, sure," the big guy assured him.

The two guys took their skates and headed for the customer benches.

Mike picked up the phone and dialed Ernie in the office.

"Yeah, Ernie speaking," was the answer.

"This is Mike. Two guys came in drunk and rented skates. They might cause trouble. Just thought I'd warn you."

"I'll be right out," replied Ernie.

～

Ernie walked up to the counter and asked, "Where are they?"

"They went to the benches to put on the skates. They might be out on the ice now," replied Mike. "I bet they fall on their ass."

"Thanks," said Ernie as he turned and left.

～

Ernie went looking and saw the two drunks out on the ice. They were staggering around and causing some congestion. The other skaters were trying to stay out of their way. Ernie went over to where they were trying to maneuver around.

"Excuse me fellas, but you're liable to fall and get hurt in your condition," he warned them.

"Aw, we're fine, don't worry," answered the big one.

"No, you guys better come on off the ice," insisted Ernie. "Somebody's going to get hurt. Take off your skates and we'll give you your money back."

Ernie went out to where the drunks were and tried to take them off the ice. The pair was giving Ernie a rough time, pushing him away.

One of the spectators came over to the rental counter and told Mike that Ernie was in a scuffle with two drunk guys. Mike took the money drawer and hid it in a bin behind some skates. He took off out the side door and ran out to the ice looking for the troublemakers. A small crowd was standing and watching Ernie struggling with the two drunks. Mike trotted to the spot of the melee and grabbed the big guy from behind pulling him off the ice, sitting him down of the floor. Ernie looked at them and then at the smaller guy. The smaller guy wasn't quite as drunk and came off the ice, voluntarily. Mike held tightly to the guy's jacket sleeves from behind to keep him on the floor. Ernie came over and told both guys to take off their skates, pronto. The guy on the floor seemed bewildered by it all and just sat there. Ernie bent down and untied the guy's skates and pulled them off. He ordered the other guy to take his off. With the skates off, Ernie told the guy, "Go get your shoes and your pal's shoes and get out of here or else we'll call the cops."

When the guy came back with the shoes, Mike and Ernie lifted up the big guy and guided him to the exit and forced him outside. The smaller guy went out too.

"Don't try to come back in or I'll call the cops and they'll put you both in jail!" Ernie warned them.

Ernie dusted himself off and told Mike, "Thanks, Skates. You better get back to the counter."

༄

Mike went back to the rental room and started to take in the returning skates. He went inside the bin where the drawer was hidden and took it back to the counter. The wall clock said 10:45. It was almost closing time. A few more late skaters brought back their skates when Ernie turned the lights off and on to signal the rink was closing. Mike worked fast tying pairs together and returning them to the proper bins. Finally, he opened the cash drawer and counted the money. There was $155 in the drawer. That meant the rental receipts was $120. Only 30 pair were rented out. It was a slow night, money wise. He closed the cash drawer and took it into the office.

"Here's the cash, Ernie," said Mike.

"Put it down here," motioned Ernie.

"Kind of quiet tonight," commented Mike.

"Un huh," replied Ernie. "Mostly."

"Uh, you want to show me how to sharpen?" asked Mike.

After a moment, Ernie got up from his chair and led Mike into the workroom. He picked up a pair of skates and turned on the grinder.

"Watch this," he told Mike.

He held one skate, blade towards the grinder and rolled it down the skate against the flat of the blade. He was sharpening the edges of the blades in doing this.

"You only do this once or twice to each skate," he told Mike. "You don't want to overdo it and put a notch in the blade."

"I get it," acknowledged Mike.

"Here, you do the other skate and I'll watch you," said Ernie, holding out the skate.

Mike took the skate and ran it lightly against the wheel.

"Do it a little harder," instructed Ernie. "You want to put an edge on the sides of the blade. That gives it the sharp tonality."

Mike ran it a second time trying to not to push too hard. He showed it to Ernie.

"How's this?" he asked.

Ernie inspected the blade and gave it a quick pass against the grinder. He handed it to Mike and said, "See how you want it to look?"

"I get it," said Mike, giving the skate back to Ernie.

"Now do a pair by yourself and then we'll call it a night," said Ernie.

Mike sharpened another pair of figure skates and got the nod from Ernie.

"You're all ready, Skates," declared Ernie. "I'll let you know when I need you to sharpen."

Mike put on his baseball cap and turned to go.

"Thanks for your quick response with those drunk guys, Skates. Next time anyone acting funny tries to rent skates, give me a call first."

"Okay, boss," replied Mike going out the door. "G'night."

Chapter 18
Academics

Mike listened as the American Lit teacher, Miss Hollingsworth, bounced around the classroom asking students about John Steinbeck's *Grapes of Wrath* novel.

"Why do you think Steinbeck wanted Joad to get arrested in the story?" she asked the kids.

"Just to show how mean our policemen were back in those days," answered one girl.

"How about you, Evelyn? What do you think?" she asked.

"I think the police were pretty much used to doing things forcefully back in the "dust bowl" days and they liked to demonstrate their toughness to the civilians who were at their mercy," she opined.

"Mister Thomas," the teacher addressed Mike, as she walked down the aisle towards him. "What's your take?"

"I think Steinbeck was a product of the thought climate of the times that wanted to demonstrate and inform us of how unfair and desperate the situation was for the migrant workers," answered Mike.

Miss Hollingsworth stood looking at Mike for a moment.

"It looks like you don't just get into the story, Mike, but look at the author's purpose, too."

"Kind of," replied Mike. "I think all writers have an agenda."

"That's true," admitted the teacher, as she walked back to the front of the room.

Mike looked around the room for some show of feed back from the other students.

"And how do the rest of you feel about John Steinbeck?" the teacher asked.

❧

Spanish 4 class was into heavy conversation aspects of the language and some of the contemporary slang showing up. Mike noticed that a lot of English language, neuvo, high-tech words were being incorporated into the Spanish dialog. Mike was at the point now where he could converse with Hispanics, as long as they didn't talk too fast. There were a few Spanish speaking kids in school that he would exchange greetings with. Sometimes Mike would comment in Spanish to them. He felt comfortable in coming to this class.

❧

Lunchtime for Mike was study time, not socializing time. He sat down on a bench by himself and broke out his notepad or a textbook while he was eating. Some of his swim team buddies would stop by to say, "hi", but Mike would go back to his schoolwork after he acknowledged them. The only time he would stop studying was when his hockey pals stopped by. Sometimes, some admiring female would walk by and say, "Hi".

"Hi, yourself," he would answer them. Or, "You're looking good!" he would say. The females were a big distraction for him because he was compelled to look them over when they walked by.

❧

Fifth period Civics was another class he had to focus on. There was a lot to government at state and local levels as well as at the federal level. He got to a point to where he understood the mechanics of government but hadn't enough time to follow the ongoing politics. His mom and dad were conservative, whereas his sister was slightly liberal, she being influenced by the university attitudes. At any rate, Civics, while not a state requirement, was interesting to him. It would help him out when and if he went to law school, as was the plan. All in all, calculus was the big concern of his curriculum. He would have to get with Wisner about it when he got the chance.

✥

End of day swimming was taking a big toll on Mike's existence. It was the way of all varsity sports, with all their demands. He would come home late every afternoon. His skin was becoming very dry from all that time in the water.

✥

Upcoming graduation was putting pressure on all the seniors to get their requirements in order, with photos, rehearsals, and such. The senior prom was rearing its eternal head into the picture. It was a big thing for a lot of people, especially, the girls. And he still had to apply at some college before it was too late.

Chapter 19
Library Encounter

Mike and Herb Wisner had planned some study sessions for late in the term for the final exams. They shared two classes, as mentioned earlier, calculus and civics. On a Saturday morning late in May, they walked into the Laketown Municipal Library for the first of these sessions.

"I see you're not wearing that cast any more," commented Mike. "How's your arm?"

"I'm all better. No pain or stiffness at all," he replied. "It was actually a bad stress fracture. Everything was still in place."

"Here, let's sit over there in the study section where we can talk," said Mike.

They wended their way into a corner section of the library, pulled out some chairs and sat down at a heavy table. They laid their textbooks on the table.

"Now, we're gonna prepare ourselves for getting top grades," exclaimed Mike. "You can get an A without these study sessions, Wiz. I'm the guy who is most benefiting from this meeting."

"Not necessarily," replied Wisner. "Talking things over with you helps me understand things better. Don't sell yourself short," he countered.

Wisner sat with his back to the wall shelf. He looked over Mike's shoulder and saw their fellow senior classmate, Jennifer Lundberg, at the far end of the room.

"Don't look now but Jennifer Lundberg is here in back of you," he said.

"No kidding," said Mike, turning around. "Stay here, Wiz. I'm going to bring her over. She's smart as hell. She's in our calculus class. Maybe she can help us out. I mean help me out, ha, ha. I'm not kidding."

Mike walked over to where Jennifer was sitting, reading a library book.

"Hi Jennifer," he said, sitting down next to her.

"Oh, Mike, hi. What are you doing here? I thought you worked on Saturday."

"I'm here studying with Wisner. I don't work Saturdays anymore."

"Oh, I see," she replied.

"Come on over to where we're sitting," he said. "We're going to talk about calculus."

She looked at him for a moment, then got up with her book and said, "Okay, let's go."

Mike smiled at this bit of good fortune as he walked with her to his table. He knew she was acing calculus.

She sat down across from Mike, next to Wisner.

"Hi, Herb," she greeted him. "I'm here."

Wisner stood up politely and nodded to her, then sat back down. "Hi Jennifer. Thanks for coming over."

"Well, what about calculus?" she asked, smiling through her heavy framed glasses.

"Mike needs our help with differentials," he explained.

She looked across at Mike and said, "You've got to think logically and the purpose of knowing calculus. It's a lot about changes in conditions like time."

They went into the mechanics of some of the equations and the results of the solutions.

"Yeah, I kind of get it," said Mike.

"Here. Work out this equation and see what it tells you," she said.

After some intense computations, Mike came up with the answer. "Aha!" he exclaimed.

"You see," she asked.

"Yeah, I see. I guess I have to trust myself to understand this process."

After awhile, Wisner suggested they talk over civics. Mike lay down his hand calculator and said, "I'm ready for that."

"Are you taking civics?" Wisner asked Jennifer.

"I took it last semester," she replied.

"Oh, so you know this stuff," he exclaimed.

"I've read the Constitution a half dozen times," said Mike. "I'm having a hard time remembering the numbering of the articles. Knowing the reasoning behind them is important, I mean for the final exam."

"Take each one at a time," said Jennifer. "Then you'll catch on. Look at the history, too."

"What about the "Declaration"?" he asked. "There's a lot more to that than people realize."

"I think I'm in touch with it," chimed in Wisner. "What's the test like, Jennifer?"

"They're going to ask the meaning of them, mostly. Know that. And don't slough over any of them," she added.

"Come on Jennifer," said Mike. "Ask us some questions."

"Okay, what's the first amendment addressing?" she asked.

"Uh, freedom of speech, you mean?" asked Mike.

"And don't forget, every state has it's own constitution. Wisconsin, too, with its legislature, judicial court system and Supreme Court, plus a governor with a cabinet," she added.

It went on with that for about forty-five minutes. They sat back after a while and called a halt with the quiz.

"What's going on with Mary Jane, Wiz?" asked Mike.

"Well, she's kind of adopted me," answered Wisner.

"I know, she kind of cares about you," said Mike, knowingly.

"Yeah, that's okay with me," he said.

"I saw her in a couple of track meets," said Mike. "She really hauls ass. She won both races in one of them."

"You going to the prom?" asked Mike.

"I'm taking her if I do go," replied Wisner. "What about you?"

"I haven't thought much about it," confessed Mike, gesturing with open palms. "I'd have to look around for a date. I dunno. I guess I'm not much for school spirit. I'm not a fun guy."

They sat quietly for a while. They both looked at Jennifer. She was looking calmly at Wisner.

No one knew much about her private life. She just didn't talk about it.

"What do you do in your spare time, Jennifer?" asked Mike. "You working?"

"Well I earn a little bit tutoring kids and classmates. I charge them a nominal fee."

"Hey, you could have charged me!" laughed Mike. "You dating anyone or hanging out with anyone? I don't pay much attention to the social relationships at school."

"No one in particular," she replied. "If you're wondering if I'm going to the prom, I don't guess I am."

"What do you think about this extracurricular school stuff?" asked Mike.

"I try not to think about it," she replied.

Mike looked at her hard for a moment. Wisner looked too. It got quiet.

"Like shit you're not!" exclaimed Mike, out of the blue.

"Like shit what?" asked Jennifer, looking puzzled.

"Like shit you're not going to the prom, I mean," replied Mike. "You're going with me."

"Are you asking me to go?" she asked, with her head tilted right.

"I'm asking you and telling you," he said. "I'm taking you to the prom, that is unless you turn me down."

Jennifer looked at Wisner and shrugged her shoulders. Wisner shrugged his shoulders, too.

"You going with anyone, Wiz?" asked Mike. "If not we can double date."

"This is kind of all of a sudden, isn't it Mike?" asked Wisner.

Mike gestured with his hands out to the side. "Maybe? It's a big deal, the prom!"

He looked at Jennifer and waved his hand slightly.

"I guess I'm not turning you down," she said, touching her right hand to her cheek, staring at him.

Mike got up from his chair and picked up his books.

"Let's go, Wiz. I'm all studied out. I have other homework, too."

He looked at Jennifer. "You need a ride or anything? We've got room."

"I don't know," she replied. "I kind of don't know what I want to do."

"How'd you get here?" asked Wisner.

"I walked. I only live two blocks away. I think I better walk," she decided, still sitting there.

Mike and Wisner walked out and headed for Mike's van.

"You ought to start lifting weights, Mike," said Wisner on the way to the van. "It helps a lot. Your body is going to need it. You've got to start young."

"Yeah, maybe," answered Mike.

Chapter 20
Prom Night

School let out early, the day of the senior prom. The girls had to get their hair done, their nails, and so forth. It was a lot of work for them. The boys had to get their suits ready, polish their shoes, and the corsage for their date. Mike was glad it was a Thursday event and not Friday when he had to work. He pedaled his bike home and took his suit out of the plastic bag. He was going to wear his dress shirt with a long glossy necktie, and dress black shoes. His hair was a little grown out but he hadn't had a recent haircut. "Too bad about that," he muttered. He shaved off his two-day growth of beard and got out his dress black shoes and sox. His suit was dark blue and looked almost black like a navy uniform. He showered quickly and put on his underwear. He walked downstairs and asked his mom,

"Is the van gassed up?"

"And washed," answered his mom.

"Great!" he exclaimed. "I'm all set."

"What about a flower for your date?" she asked.

"Oh boy," he said. "What'll I get her?"

"Get a gardenia, Mike," she advised him. "It works."

*

Herb Wisner was really nervous. He didn't know whether to lift his dumbbells before getting ready. His right arm needed the work.

"Aw, the heck with it!" he decided.

He got cleaned up, shaved and looked over his wardrobe. He thought about the plan of going with Mike to the prom and then coming home to get his dad's car afterwards to go partying. They both thought it was best to be alone with their dates after the dance.

His mom came into the bedroom and looked over the situation.

"You should have seen your dad dressed up in his uniform when he took me dancing before we got married," she said.

"Yeah, Mom. I believe you. I'm sure dad looked extra sharp."

"Are you bringing this Mary Jane around so we can see her?" she demanded.

"Sure thing, Mom, for sure!"

"I gotta get dressed Mom," he told her. "I can't be yakking with you."

He put on his clothes, carefully, making sure his necktie was well tied.

After he put on his shoes, he went over to the closet door mirror to see how he looked. He was surprised at how good looking he was. He grinned this way and that to see how he looked, smiling.

※

Mary Jane was somewhat concerned about looking right for this dance. She wasn't used to wearing evening clothes. Her mom had gone with her to pick out a dress and some matching high-heeled shoes. She would use her mom's small purse. Her mom had done her hair for her. She borrowed her mom's makeup to put on. After her shower she got dressed. The clothes fit her well. She had the right kind of figure that made anything look good on her. She had a cloth coat that would do quite well. So it turned out she didn't have to worry about her appearance. She knew Wisner already liked her looks. Looking in the full-length mirror she was surprise at how tall she looked in heels. Luckily, Wisner was tall enough to compensate for her height.

※

In their apartment two blocks north of Lake Street, Jennifer Lundberg and her mother were working on shaping her up for the big event. Her mother, Betty Ann, was a medical assistant at the Laketown Hospital. She was very professional and very familiar with the latest fashions in womens' clothes. She was divorced from Jennifer's father who was a doctor in Madison. She had been very attractive in her youth and Jennifer had inherited some of her traits.

They had gone to some of the local shops to pick out a dress for Jennifer. They had chosen a smart looking pair of high-heeled shoes to go with the dress. Her mother had always preached good grooming to her daughter but Jennifer showed little interest in smart looking clothes. Jennifer did prefer wearing dresses over the pants look adopted by most other girls her age. Her mom did succeed in getting Jennifer into changing her hairstyle a little to give her a different look for a special event.

"Are you going to wear your glasses tonight?" she asked Jennifer.

"I don't know, mom," she answered. "I don't have to, I guess. I'm not that blind."

"Take 'em off and put some makeup on your frame markings. Give your escort a break. He wants you to look as best you can. What's this guy like?"

"He's looks okay, plenty okay," replied Jennifer. "He's into sports, but he takes college prep classes."

He mom looked at her hard and said, "I'm really glad you're going to the prom. It's a big deal after the dust settles. You never forget it."

"I'm lucky to be going, mom," she confessed.

※

Mike pulled away from the flower shop. He had picked up an extra gardenia for Wisner to give to his date. He headed for Jennifer's place since it was close by. It was 5:45 PM, still early. He looked at the house numbers when he got close. He stopped in front of her apartment, a three story building. She lived on the second floor. He jumped out of his car patting down his hair. It was now a couple of inches long. He pressed her doorbell to let him into the building.

"Come on up, Mike," the voice announced. The front door lock opened with a click. He took the stairs instead of the elevator. When he got to her unit, the door was ajar. He pushed it open.

"How did you know it was me?" he asked.

"I looked out the window," she said.

She stood in front of him, one hand on the other wrist. She looked happy, he decided.

"This is my mom. Her name is Betty Ann," she said with a smile.

"How do you do?" said Mike, reaching out his right hand, "Uh, Betty Ann. I'm Mike Thomas. My dad owns the lumberyard on Lakefront Street," he said , nervously. "Oh, this is for you, a gardenia," he added, handing it to Jennifer. "I don't know where you pin it."

Her mother stepped up and took his hand. She smiled at him, indicating her approval.

"Jennifer says you're into sports," she said. "Are you a ballplayer?"

"No, I'm on the swim team," he replied.

"He plays hockey, too," chimed in Jennifer.

"I'm happy to know you, Mike," said her mother.

"Same to you, Ma'am," replied Mike.

Mike looked at Jennifer. She looked plenty good tonight. "Huh," he thought to himself.

"You want to go?" he asked her. "We're picking up Wisner and his date."

"Wisner plays hockey, too, Mom," she informed her mother.

"Well, you young people have a good time," said her mother.

They took the stairs down, Mike holding her hand.

He opened the door for her to get into the front seat and closed it afterwards. He came around to the driver's side and let himself in. He clicked his belt and she followed suit.

"I almost don't recognize you," he admitted.

"My mom transformed me," she said.

"She's got the touch," said Mike, as he pulled the van out into the traffic lane.

At the first red light, Mike said, "This is a lot different isn't it. I mean, me taking you out."

"Don't be nervous, Mike. I'm the one who should be."

⚜

They turned down Shoreview Street and Mike parked at the curb in front of a modest frame house.

"This is Wisner's house," said Mike. "I'll get him. Uh, you wanta come along?"

"He opened her door and they went to the front door together. A silver Toyota was parked in the driveway. Mike rang the doorbell. Herb Wisner opened the door.

"Come in amigos," he said.

Mike was surprised to see Mary Jane was already there.

"Hi MJ," said Mike, taking her hand. "Glad you could make it," he laughed.

The two girls looked at each other. They had never met.

"Meet Jennifer Lundberg," said Mike.

"Hi," they exchanged greetings. Apparently, they had never seen each other before.

Wisner's parents and little sister came into the room and were all introduced.

"Oh this is fun!" said Wilma, Wisner's mother. "Getting us all together like this."

Wisner's dad nodded and smiled at the group.

After all the formalities, the two couples went out to Mike's van, for the night, and got in, with Wisner and Mary Jane in the back.

"Listen, you guys," explained Mike. "I have to stop by my house. My mom and dad want to see who all's going and stuff. So just hang in there. We'll make it to the prom soon enough."

They drove to Mike's house, a short five minute drive and all got out of the van. Mike rang the doorbell so as to alert his parents.

His dad met them at the door and said, "Hello, what can I do for you?"

They all laughed and went into the front room.

"This is all of us," said Mike. "What do ya think?"

"You're all beautiful!" exclaimed Mike's mother. "Thanks for stopping by."

She shook hands with everyone. Mike's dad, Bill, did the same. He had never met the girls before. All of a sudden, Mike felt very young. He looked at he clock on the table.

"We better go, now," he declared. "It's 6:35."

They all said their goodbyes and went back to the van. Mike and Wisner opened the doors, politely, and they all buckled up inside.

"I have to admit to you all that this is a weird experience for me," said Mike, as he drove to the schoolyard.

"Me too," said Wisner. "You aren't alone."

The girls were quiet all the way to the prom.

Mike passed his second gardenia to Wisner over his shoulder and they all laughed. Mary Jane told him where to pin it.

⁂

They pulled into the schoolyard parking lot and Mike parked in a space away from the other cars. He didn't want to get any dents in his mom's van. Nobody complained. They got out of the van and walked calmly to the front entrance of the school gym. The boys held the girls hands on the way. Mary Jane looked tall even next to Wisner who was 6 foot one.

The band was warming up making weird sounds on their instruments. The two couples made their way to a row of chairs against the wall and sat down. Mike had a feeling that they were being scrutinized by the other students. He knew nobody expected him to bring Jennifer. Nobody even expected him to come to the prom. Wisner was another story. He and Mary Jane were already an item.

"Are we drinking punch tonight, Mike?" asked Wisner.

"I haven't decided yet," replied Mike.

A few minutes later, the band struck up the first dance number. It was a slow one. The two couples got up and started dancing. Mike put his arm around Jennifer and held the other out front and they started moving. She seemed to follow okay so he felt safe with this one. He had never touched her like this before. Her legs looked damn good, he noticed. Mary Jane had runner's legs so you expected hers to look shapely. How they could move in those high heels was a mystery to Mike. After a couple of numbers, the band stopped playing and the school principal made a speech from in front of the bandstand.

"Welcome to the graduating class of Spring 2018," he started out. After that he cited a few things special things about the class and introduced some of the teachers and advisors, etc., etc., and everyone clapped. When he finished his speech, he bid everyone a good time and a goodbye. Everyone clapped again.

The band picked up with a fast one and Mike asked Jennifer, "What do we do?"

"Just kind of walk around fast. It's all the same stuff."

"How do you know all about dancing?" he asked her.

"Oh I practiced a little at home when I knew I was coming," she replied, shrugging her shoulders. "Just don't kick me!" she cautioned him.

She and Mike started moving their feet around like everyone else, careful not to get tangled up with other dancers. Mike had done this before in middle school so he wasn't a stranger to it. This went on for a while until Jennifer suggested they sit down. They went to the side wall looking for a couple of empty seats and sat down.

"I'm going to get us a couple of drinks," said Mike. "What are you drinking?"

"Get me a small 7 up," she replied.

He hustled over to the bar and got the drinks served in cups by a bartender. He took them back to the seats and handed her one and sat down.

"Are we having fun?" asked Mike, with his eyebrows raised?

She broke out laughing hard, and said, "This is what dances are like. You go out and dance and the more you like dancing, the more fun you're having, ha, ha."

"Yeah," chuckled Mike. "I get it."

After a few minutes, they got up again and did another fast one. This went on until the band stopped and took a break. They went looking for seats and spotted Wisner and Mary Jane and sat down next to them.

"This is a blast!" exclaimed Mike. "Don't ya think?"

Wisner and Mary Jane gave a few long ha, ha's.

Some more school administrators got up with some more words of encouragement during the break. There was a lot of laughing and conversation going on. Eventually, Donny Smith came over escorting one of his girlfriends and said "Hi" to them. Mike introduced him to Jennifer and they talked about classes together. Then Bobby Rockford came over with another girl that Mike had seen around a few times. The girls heard all about some of the hockey stuff the boys had in common.

The dance music started up again with a slow one and Mike and Jennifer got up for it. He liked this because he got to hold her close to him. After a while, he spotted Evelyn Jurgenson dancing close by with her boyfriend Johnny. They nodded to each other and Evelyn gave Jennifer a long hard look.

"Nice dance, huh?" Mike said to Evelyn.

She smiled and nodded "Yes" to him again as they drifted apart. Johnny never spoke.

It was getting a little tiresome for Mike, since this wasn't his lifestyle. The two couples sat down together and started talking about their college plans. Mary Jane said she would run track but wasn't sure about hockey. Mike and Wisner swore on the bible that they would keep skating. Jennifer said that she was going to study hard and get an advanced degree. Wisner told her to start working out with weights to stay in good shape. He admonished Mike about it, too. As it turned out they had a good time talking to each other.

Mike looked at Jennifer tonight and thought to himself she was damn good looking. He had known her a long time from different classes they were in together but they never got close. He liked her voice and the way she enunciated her words. Her heavy rimmed glasses seemed to be a deterrent. They kind of kept you at arms length from her.

Mike looked at his watch. It was after 10:00. People were starting to leave. There were some other parties that people were going to where there would some liquor to be had. Mike always worried about the kids smoking Marijuana. That was a turn off for him. He whispered to Wisner, "What do you want to do?"

"We can get out of here," advised Wisner. "Take me to my house. I've got keys to the family car."

"Okay," said Mike. "Let's go."

Mike got up and stretched a little. Wisner got up too. The girls looked at them and knew it was time to go.

"Time's up girls," said Mike. "They're going to shut down this place pretty soon."

The girls got up and went to the rest room. Mike and Wisner went to the boy's bathroom. When they all came out the band was playing a "Good Night" song. Mike took Jennifer in his arms and they danced a few steps and started to laugh. Then they walked out the exit and headed out to the car.

Chapter 21
After the Prom

Mike pulled into Wisner's driveway behind the family car. Wisner got out of the car and helped Mary Jane get out. Mike turned off the car's ignition and got out on the driver's side. He walked over to Wisner and spoke to him quietly.

"You know where you're going, Wiz? You're not going to just cruise around are you?"

"I figured we would just go over to the lake and park," he answered.

"You ready for that?" asked Mike.

"Uh, yeah, uh, I don't know," replied Wisner.

"Just remember how old you and Evans are," advised Mike.

Mike walked back to the van and called out, "We're going over to the Yogurt Station. After that, who knows?"

Mike shut the door behind him and buckled his belt. He turned to Jennifer.

"What do you want to do?"

"I was thinking, go to the Yogurt Station," she replied, looking out the window.

Mike started laughing. "I guessed right, didn't I."

She laughed too. Mike started the car and backed out of the driveway and drove towards Lake Street.

⁂

"I think those two are really in love," said Jennifer, breaking the silence.

"You're right about that, lady," replied Mike. "He was smitten, the day she showed up for hockey practice."

"You called me lady!" she exclaimed. "You think I'm a very mature person."

"Yeah, I guess I do," admitted Mike. "I really don't know what to do with you. I thought we should talk. We don't really know each other."

"I didn't hear what you said to Wisner, but I'm guessing it was a word of caution," she answered.

"That's what it was," admitted Mike.

"You're pretty mature, yourself, Mike," she suggested.

"My mom talks to me a lot about life and relationships," said Mike.

❧

Mike pulled into the Yogurt Station parking lot and found a space towards the back end.

"Hmm," he commented. "It looks like the whole town is here. Let's go in."

He opened the door for her, closed it and locked the van. They walked slowly to the side door and went in. After a moment, they found an empty table near the front window. He looked across the table at his date in the bright light. She looked younger than before. He looked around the room and noticed some of the kids from the prom.

"Who goes first?" he asked her. "Me or you?"

"I'll go first," she said. "Don't go away," she smiled at him.

Mike put the car keys into his jacket pocket.

"Not a chance, I'm going away," he muttered to himself.

A few minutes later, she came back with her cup and he got up to serve himself. He picked a pistachio and vanilla mix.

He took both cups to the cash register and paid the clerk. He gave Jennifer her yogurt and sat down.

"Wow!" he exclaimed. "They charge 40 cents an ounce."

"Did you pay cash or your credit card?" she asked.

"I paid cash," he said.

"Any post mortems?" she inquired.

"Yeah," he said. "I'm glad as hell I took you."

She nodded, "Thanks for taking me."

He ate his yogurt quickly then pushed aside his cup. She ate slowly and looked around the room.

"You know anyone here?" he asked.

"They're looking at us, a few of them, it seems. We don't look like a likely couple," she observed. "They're not my cronies," she answered.

"You're better looking than a lot of 'em realized," he said. "You're special. How tall are you?"

"I'm five-five," she said. "How about you?"

"You keep to yourself, I noticed," he said. "Oh I'm six foot."

"I don't think I want to be popular. It doesn't get you anywhere."

"I've always assumed that you thought well of me. You were always friendly," Mike said.

"I felt good around you," she replied.

Mike looked at the wall clock. It was 11:30.

"It's just about my bedtime," interjected Mike. "Do you want to go?"

They both got up.

≈

Wisner had taken Mary Jane to Shadow Lake and saw other cars parked there. He pulled up to the concrete sea wall. He opened his side window slightly and turned the key off.

"This is the go to place," he mused.

They looked at each other.

"I love you," he told her. "I don't know what to do about that."

"I love you too," she replied.

"We're kids, you know, I've been reminded," said Wisner. "We both live at home."

She nodded, "Yes. I know."

She leaned forward in her seat and took off her coat. Wisner moved close to her and kissed her on the mouth. She put her arms around him and kissed him back.

"How come you love me?" she asked him.

"I fell in love with you, early on, when you joined the team," he said. "When I saw you running track, I was a little bit overwhelmed, but I got over it. You look beautiful to me."

"If we go to college together, I know we'll be sleeping together," he pointed out.

Her arms were still around his neck. They kissed again.

"Jesus, you feel good!" he whispered, feeling her breasts against him.

"You do too," she whispered back. "You're good looking too."

Wisner reached down to the seat adjustment bar and pushed his seat back. He reached down and pushed her seat back, also. He let down his release break. She kicked off her shoes and slid backwards over the gearbox onto his lap. She slowly put her arms around his neck. He held her close to him and they were locked in a tight embrace. A few seconds later, he put his hand inside her dress and between her thighs and up her leg. She took his wrist and moved his hand up inside her underpants. She was breathing hard and moving his around hand in a circular motion. His fingers felt the wetness of the spot and he kept up the motion. Thirty seconds later she let out a moan and stiffened her body. After a moment she relaxed and started sobbing and held him closer.

⌘

Mike had his hand on the door handle of the van about to let Jennifer in. She stood there waiting until he let go. They were in the back end of the Yogurt parking lot. He took her in his arms, put his head next to hers and hugged her. She hugged him back. He stepped back, opened the door and she sat down inside. He got in and buckled his seat belt.

"I guess it's home for us, huh?" he said.

"What can I say?" she replied.

"I wouldn't know what to say," he responded.

He drove out of the parking lot and headed for her apartment. It was about a half-mile away. He pulled up next to the curb, put the gearshift in park and turned off the engine. He gave her a quizzical look and sat back in his seat.

"The light's on in my front room," she commented.

"Maybe, your mom's waiting up?" he asked.

"I'll bet she is," laughed Jennifer.

He got out of the car and let her out the other side. He walked her to the entry door. They stopped and looked at each other.

"Hug me and kiss me goodnight," she told him.

He took her in his arms and kissed her. It was the first time for them.

"Don't let go yet," she pleaded.

"I've got you. I'm not letting go," he assured her.

He felt her body close to him. She had a good figure from the feel of her.

"Man!" he thought to himself. "What am I going to do about her?" "When's your birthday?" he asked her.

"It's in October. You don't have to get me a present," she chided him.

"Mine is in September," he said. "I'm glad I'm older than you."

"Hooray!" she cheered. "I'm out with an older guy."

They were quiet for a minute.

"What are we going to do about us?" he asked.

"No much now, I'm afraid," she replied. "I'm going to go to university, get a degree, then on to grad school, for sure."

"I know that," he said. "Can I see you over the summer or are we all done?"

"You're an athlete, Mike," she explained. "I'm an egghead. We're going to have different lifestyles. I can't afford to mess around and get involved and pregnant. If I keep seeing you, I'm going to love you more than I already do."

"I am really liking you, now," said Mike. "I just don't feel like dropping you all of a sudden."

She reached up and kissed him again. After a minute, she said,

"Tell you what. I'm going to come back to Laketown in four or five years and if I'm not already attached, I'm going to come looking for you. If you're already attached, it'll be tough luck for me."

"You're on," agreed Mike. "I'll walk you upstairs."

"You don't have to. I'm okay."

"No. I'm not going to leave you down here. I want to leave a good impression on your mom."

She let herself in on the lock pad near the door and it clicked open. It clicked shut behind them as the climbed the stairs to the second floor. Jennifer knocked lightly on the door. There was no response. She took out her door key and let them in. Her mom was dozing on the davenport. She opened her eyes when they came in. She sat up quickly.

"Oh hi, you kids. I guess I dozed off reading this book (on the floor next to her)."

"Hi mom," she said. "Mike brought me home."

"Hello, again, uh, missus, uh, Betty Ann," said Mike.

Her mom had light brown hair and was still attractive. "Oh it's only midnight," she noted. "Was it fun?" she inquired.

Mike raised his two thumbs in the affirmative.

"It was big fun, Mom," replied Jennifer. "We even danced."

Her mom looked hard at Mike.

"You're a good looking guy, Mike," she said. "What are you going to be when you grow up?" she smiled.

"I'm looking to becoming a lawyer," he said.

"Are you going to keep playing hockey?" she asked.

"I'm afraid so, ma'am," he replied.

Mike stood for a moment.

"I'll see you in school, Jennifer. "Thanks for going with me."

"Thanks, Mike," she said as she gave him a hug.

Then he was out the door.

≪

After he left, Jennifer sat down with her mom. There were tears in her eyes.

"What's wrong, baby?" asked her mom. "Did something happen?"

"Oh I just had the best experience of my life," she said, looking up at the ceiling. "It was a big deal. I'll never forget this night. I mean going to the senior prom. I guess it was meant to be."

Mother and daughter hugged each other.

Chapter 22
Graduation

Laketown High School Commencement was set for June 14. It would be an outdoor event as usual, held in the football stadium. The Monday before, the seniors were presented their caps and gowns for the ceremony. This year they would be black for the boys and orange for the girls. On Tuesday they marched through the parade route to the ever enduring, *Pomp and Circumstance* tune. It was a time of mixed feelings. There was the feeling of thanks for achievement and the feel of melancholy in leaving your friends. On Tuesday's rehearsal, Mike spied Jennifer waiting in the grandstands after the diploma march. He took off his cap and trudged over to where she was sitting. She smiled at him when he got close to her. He climbed up two rows of seats and stood looking down at her.

"I see you made it," he congratulated her. "Nice going."

"Thanks. The same to you," she replied.

He sat down next to her to speak quietly.

"I know you don't want to get too involved with me but I want you to go out with me after the big event, Thursday."

"My mom wants me to hang out with her right afterwards. What about later in the evening?" she responded.

"Are we double dating again?" she asked.

"I don't think so. I didn't make any plans. Most people are hanging out with their families."

"What about your parents?" she asked.

"Well, my sister is home. We haven't talked about it. They'll be at the ceremony."

"What time?" she asked.

"I'll take you to dinner, about 7:30," he said.

"I'm glad you're working and can afford me," she said.

"Hey, I make twenty-five a week at the rink. I don't blow it!" he exclaimed.

They sat for a while, watching the panorama evolving in front of them.

"I was accepted at Wisconsin, River Falls," he said to her. "It's upstate. I think I'll go there."

"That's great!" she said. "That sounds good. What's your major going to be?"

"Could be econ or political science," he replied. "Or maybe history."

"How about you? Where are you going?" he asked.

"I was accepted at two schools," she replied. "I think I'll study biology. What do you think of pharmacology?"

"You can open your own drugstore."

The students started going back to their classes. Jennifer stood up and took off her cap and gown and folded them under her arm. Mike stood up.

"Which way you going?" he asked.

"I'm going to my Latin class," she replied. "Let's walk."

꧂

Mike walked into his American Lit class and sat down. There was only fifteen minutes left before the bell rang. The teacher looked up and nodded. Most in the class were seniors like Mike. The teacher, Miss Hollingsworth, had graded the tests taken the previous Friday. She passed them out, individually, walking around the room. They were in old-fashioned blue book form. Mike opened the blue cover and looked at the grade on the first page. He got an "A". There was a note alongside the grade. It read, *"You've got a good feel for literature, Mike"*. The essay he had written was about the thinking of Mark Twain when he wrote the Huck Finn story. On the way out when the bell rang, Mike thanked the teacher for the class. She looked pleased.

In Spanish class, the teacher asked everyone a question in Spanish, to which they would have to answer in Spanish. Then she would ask another question with the same requirement in reply. She walked around the room doing this.

At lunch break, Mike looked for Wisner. He found him sitting with Blakely near the cafeteria.

"No Mary Jane, today?" asked Mike.

"She told me I was getting boring," he laughed.

"What are you up to Blake?" asked Mike.

"I'm getting bored talking to Wisner," he laughed.

"You gonna keep playing goalkeeper?" Mike asked.

"I think I'm getting good at it," he replied.

Mike opened his sack and found a veggie wrap wrapped in foil and an apple. He showed it to his friends.

"My mom's out to make me a vegetarian," he lamented.

He took a bite. It tasted good. "Huh," he commented.

"Hey, Wiz, you ready for Civics?" asked Mike. "I think I'm getting an "A".

"Me too," said Wisner.

"How do you guys feel about graduating? You glad or sad?" asked Blakely.

"I'm okay with it," said Mike. "I'll survive. I'm regretting leaving you guys, my teammates, though."

They looked at Wisner.

"I don't feel much of anything about that. I'm going to like going to college, though. You're more on you own," he said.

"Big question, Wiz - which school?" asked Mike, finishing his veggie wrap.

"I've been accepted to U of W, Madison," he said. "We're waiting to hear about Mary Jane."

"You guys have to be together, huh?" inferred Mike.

"That's right. It's a gotta. She's looking for a track and field scholarship."

Just then, the bell sounded the end of lunch.

"C'mon. Let's go to Civics," said Mike. "See ya later, Blake."

※

On the way up the stairs to the Civics class, they caught up with Evelyn Jurgenson. They both slowed down when they caught up with her. She looked at them. She didn't say anything. Mike gave her a little wave with his free hand.

"It's been fun," he said.

She nodded back to him.

Mike whispered to Wisner that she was probably jealous of us getting an "A".

※

Mr. Fulton surprised them by showing a documentary film about the founding fathers adopting the laws of the land and the Constitution. It featured all the major characters.

When the lights went back on, Mr. Fulton asked the class to tell him what they thought about how they were created. There was a long discussion about it. At the end of the class, he got up in front of the room and told them to never forget what they had learned in his class.

"There will be a class tomorrow so you seniors are welcome to show up. I'll show another movie."

"I'll say good luck to all you seniors who don't make it back to class."

A student in the front row raised his hand. Mr. Fulton recognized the student's wish to be heard.

"Are you any relation to Robert Fulton, the guy who invented the steam boat?"

Mr. Fulton looked at the student for several seconds before he spoke.

"I try not to let anyone in on that subject. I try to keep it a secret."

Some of the students laughed at the answer given by the teacher. They applauded as they filed out of the room.

∽

"I'm going to clean out my gym locker," Mike told Wisner. "I'll see you tomorrow."

"Right," said Wisner. "You coming to school tomorrow?"

"Yeah, Why not?"

"Fulton acted like we were all going to ditch," he replied.

"I've got nothing better to do," laughed Mike.

∽

Mike headed for the gym. When he went inside, he headed for his locker. He opened it and took out his swimming suit and other paraphernalia and stuffed them into his backpack. He closed the locker and headed for the P.E. office. He looked in and saw Coach Allison sitting at his desk. He went inside. The coach looked around and saw Mike.

"Good afternoon, Thomas," he greeted Mike.

"Hello coach. I came to say goodbye."

"Thanks for being on the team," said the coach.

Mike nodded. "I enjoyed it," he replied.

He reached his hand out to shake hands. The coach responded in kind.

"Are you going to university?" asked the coach.

Mike nodded. I'm going to River Falls I think," he answered.

"Keep swimming, Thomas," said the coach.

"I will," replied Mike, gesturing goodbye with his hand.

He turned and walked out the door.

∽

The grandstands at the Laketown stadium were filling up that Thursday morning. The sun was out and the sky was filled with scattered white clouds. It was 11:00 AM. The temperature was hovering around seventy-five degrees. A slight wind was blowing the stadium flags from northwest. The graduating students were milling around the southern end of the running track dressed in their caps and gowns. A low platform and a podium stood in front of the goal posts at the south end. The school principal and several administrators stood close by, preparing to start the program. The diplomas were lying on a table close by. A microphone and a speaker were being set up by members of the sound club. A CD player sat on a table nearby.

Mike's parents and sister were seated in the stands about halfway up. Bill Thomas had put up a sign in front of his lumberyard saying *Closed till 3:00 due to graduation*. Mary Jane's parents were there close to the bottom. Arnold and Wilma Wisner were in attendance. Sister Betty Lou came along with them. Unknown to most of the attendees, Ernie Strauss, the Ice Rink manager, was there also. In one corner on the south end of the stands, sat Betty Ann Lundberg with another woman from the hospital.

The graduating class was moving to the middle of the football field. The turf looked freshly cut. The monitors were trying to position the students in an alphabetical order. Mike and Herb Wisner were standing near the back end of the line. When all was ready, the principal, a Mister Grantly, took the stand.

"Welcome to the commencement ceremony, everyone," he began.

"We have eighty-six seniors being honored today and they are the most important people in attendance. Also important are the parents, friends and other relatives of the graduates in attendance. We salute them. Many of them will be going on to colleges and universities to begin their climb to reach their career goals. Some will be apprenticing for careers in business and in the trades. We wish all of them the best that is possible in this world. I will now turn the microphone over to the class president who has a message of encouragement to his fellow students."

A girl with straight blond hair flowing beneath her orange cap took the podium.

She stood at the microphone and looked out at the lineup of diploma winners.

"My name is Rebecca Stiles. I was fortunate enough to be voted class president by my graduating comrades. We have all worked hard to get to this place and will be working even harder as we go out into the world."

She continued on with her speech for another ten minutes and received a big round of applause from the crowd at the end. The school principal returned to the podium and announced that the cap and gown people would be called to the stand in alphabetic order, which had nothing to do with grades received.

The names were called out and the students paraded up to the stand one by one. The tune *"Pomp and Circumstance"*, accompanied the procession. After receiving their diplomas, the students gathered together on the running track. Some were shaking hands with each other. When the ceremony was over, the students and people in the stands stood for the national anthem, played on the CD machine. The crowd in the stands applauded enthusiastically at the conclusion. The students were then free to visit with their friends and relatives in the stands.

❧

The hockey players in the graduating came together on the track and shook hands with each other. Some of the kids went over to congratulate Mary Jane who had become a track and field star. Mike looked around for Jennifer Lundberg. He saw her walking up into the stands to meet her mother.

Mike went over to Wisner and told him they'd get together afterwards. He then double-timed it up to the stands to see his family. They were waiting for him, grinning. His mom was the first to embrace him. He then hugged his sister, who squeezed him hard.

"What was your GPA?", she asked. "I hear you've been a study freak."

"I got a 3.5, Sis, or thereabouts."

Sister Angie was five foot six, brown hair, good looking like her mom, and had a good figure. She would be a senior in college next semester. He then hugged his dad and shook hands with him. Some of the people around them came over to pay their respects. One of them was Ernie, his manager at the rink. Mike introduced him to his family. After talking it over with his admirers, he looked around to see who was around. He saw Wisner and called out to him. On the second try, Wisner turned around to look and waved. Mike grabbed his sister's hand and took her down to meet the Wisners.

"My sister came home from school to watch," he said.

Wisner shook hands with her. "Nice meeting you, for sure," said Wisner.

"Wow!" exclaimed Mrs. Wisner, Wilma. "You really are stunning looking!"

"I'm just a plain girl," assured Angie, smiling.

Wisner's dad, Arnold Wisner, shook her hand and smiled. Mike told Herb Wisner that he would give him a call when things got settled down.

"You ought to say "hi" to Mary Jane's family, if they're still here," he commented.

"Damn good idea," said Wisner. "Take care."

∽

Mike picked up his family and reminded them they were going to lunch. They headed down the steps and out of the stadium. Mike took off his cap and gown and tossed them into a special bin. They went out to his mom's van sitting in the parking lot.

"Where're we eating?" asked Mike. "At home, ha, ha."

"As a matter of fact, no," replied his mom. "We're going to the Howard Johnson hotel."

"Boy, we're gonna splurge!" exclaimed Mike.

"You're a special guy, Mike," said his mom.

"We're all special, Mom," said Mike.

Mike's dad, Bill, steered the van out of the lot and into the street. They were about seven minutes away from the hotel.

Chapter 23
Graduation Night

He had to call Jennifer about tonight. He wanted to verify their date for dinner. When the family got home, his dog came over to him, wagging his tail hard. He hugged him and patted his head. They had dropped dad off at the lumberyard on the way home. Mike went into the kitchen and leaned his backside against the counter. He had to stop and think about being out of school with summer coming up. He had talked over his choice of schools with his parents and his sister. They all thought that River Falls sounded okay and affordable, even though it was way upstate. They did have a hockey program. He had to check on the ROTC issue. This was going to be a whole new life for him.

His mom and sister were out in the backyard sitting on lawn chairs. He went over to the wall phone and dialed Jennifer. The phone rang three times and then heard a voice.

"Hello," a woman answered.

"Hi, this is Mike. Is Jennifer there?"

"Hi Mike, this is her mother. Congratulations. I'll get her."

"Thanks," said Mike.

A few moments later, he heard Jennifer's voice.

"Hi," she answered. "You didn't forget."

"No way," he said. "I'll come over and pick you up at 7:30."

"You don't have to take me out Mike. You don't have to buy me dinner."

"We'll go somewhere. I won't spend a lot," said Mike.

"You can come over here and we'll sit around," she suggested.

"After dinner we'll do that. We can talk about our school plans," he said.

"Okay. Do I have to get dressed?" she asked.

"Wear what you look good in," he said. "Don't get flashy."

"Okay, bye," she said.

"Bye," said Mike and hung up.

∽

Mike had the pickup truck. His dad had come home early. Mike drove to Jennifer's apartment and made a U turn and parked in front. He jumped out and went up the steps to press the intercom.

"It's me," he answered when he heard her voice."

The door clicked open. He went in and up the stairs and knocked. Jennifer opened the door and he went in. Somehow, he didn't feel self-conscious coming here. He looked at her and hugged her.

"Nice going at school," he said.

"Nice going to you, too," she countered.

"Where's Betty Ann?" he inquired.

"She's in the bedroom. She'll be out. She likes you."

"I like her, too," he said. "What did you guys do after the ceremony?"

"We went to the Waffles and Flapjacks café," she said. "We had a salad."

"We went to the Howard Johnson," said Mike. "My sister's here."

"Oh my," she said. "I'll bet she's doing good at school."

"Yeah, don't worry about her. We've got her trained."

～

Jennifer's mother came out and shook Mike's hand. Mike gave her a quick hug and thanked her.

"Thanks for being our friend," said her mother.

"Uh, yeah, uh. You're welcome," Mike stuttered, a little bit taken aback.

"We're going out to talk and stuff, Mother," said Jennifer. "We'll be back early."

She took Mike's hand and walked out the door.

～

In the pickup, Mike thought hard about where to go. The Pizza World restaurant came to mind. He started the car and said, "It's the Pizza World."

When they drove up, they parked in the lot alongside the restaurant. There were a few of customers there.

They went in and found a table and sat down.

"What do ya think?" he asked her.

"It's okay," she said.

The tablecloths were checkered and the wall had pictures of different pizzas and pastas. It was clean looking and had lighting that seemed slightly dim. He looked at her and noticed she was wearing a beige coat and a pair of jeans. She looked relaxed. He liked that. She was wearing glasses but that didn't bother him.

"You look nice, tonight," he said.

Mike was wearing a light khaki jacket and gray corduroy pants. He had on his Sketcher hiking shoes that he wore just about everywhere.

"Do you want something to eat?" he asked.

She looked up at the menu selection above the back pizza ovens and shrugged her shoulders.

"I'll order a veggie pizza and we'll play around with it," he said. "Going out to lunch today kind of took away my appetite."

"Get me a drink," she said. "A diet A&W root beer."

Mike called over the waitress and placed the order.

"This is a funny way to celebrate graduation, isn't it?" he asked her.

"It's better than getting drunk at some party," she said.

"It's good that you came out with me," said Mike. "It's not a good night to be alone. No memories."

"Thanks for taking me out, Michael," she said. "I'll remember it."

She studied him as he looked at the takeout counter. The waitress brought a large A&W with a straw.

"Thanks," said Mike.

"You don't go out that much do you, Mike?" she inquired. "You're a good looking guy and you would think that you had a few girl friends."

"You're my girlfriend tonight. I made up my mind I was going to get good grades, so I studied a lot. It paid off. I have a decent GPA."

"You flatter me, Michael," she replied. "Haven't you gotten involved with anyone in town or in school?"

"Well, don't tell anyone but had a close relationship with one of the swimmers on last year's team. She was a senior and I was junior. She kind of controlled the situation. She's long gone now. Enough said."

They looked at each other for a moment.

"Actually, you seem very mature to me," he admitted to her. "I kind of feel like you're the adult here and I'm the kid."

"But it's good you think like a grownup," he added. "Otherwise, we'd both be behaving like adolescents."

"You don't seem like a dumb kid to me, Michael," she answered. "Thank you so much for noticing me."

The waitress came to the table with the pizza. She laid it on the table with a cutting wheel on the tray.

They both thanked the waitress and looked over the veggie topping.

Mike looked down at the table and said, "I noticed you because we were in classes together. If not, we wouldn't be here tonight. We kind of built up a trust."

"This meeting is getting very serious, isn't it?" she commented.

"Well, let's eat some of the pizza, anyway," he suggested. "I can't help getting serious. That's my nature."

"Summer is starting," she said. "What are you going to do for three months?"

"I'm going to get some extra hours at the rink. I'll be doing some summer clinics and pickup games, I guess," he replied. "I have to be ready for the hockey season."

"Are you going to play up at River Falls?" she asked.

"That's the plan," he said. "Maybe swim team, too. I don't know. You ought to go with me to the rink someday. I'll teach you how to skate. You need the exercise. You can't just sit and study."

"Actually, I do exercise," she replied. "I have a rowing machine in my room and some light dumbbells. You and Wisner worry about that a lot."

"Yeah, Wisner is a weightlifter!" exclaimed Mike. "I should do weights too."

They paused their conversation and ate some of the pizza.

"Where are you going to school? Maybe you can get a scholarship. You get all A's don't you?" asked Mike.

"I've been accepted at U of W Madison and Ripon college. Ripon's a private school. Which do you think is best for me, Michael?"

"Well, either one is okay. Wisner is going to Madison, I think. What about July and August? What are you going to do?" asked Mike.

"I'm going to work in my mom's hospital doing all kinds of stuff."

She took a long sip on her soda and wiped pizza dust off her hands with a napkin. Two more couples came into the place and sat down.

"How long do you want to sit here, Jennifer?"

"Long enough to reduce the time you'll have to hold me in your arms," she joked. "Actually, that's not so funny is it?"

"That's a thought," he mused.

He took another slice of pizza and folded it part way into his mouth and took a bite.

"I have to remind myself we're still minors," he confessed to her, chewing slowly. "We're not even eighteen, yet."

Another couple came into the shop. Mike looked up and saw it was Randy McAdoo with a dark haired girl.

"Hey Mack, over here," called out Mike.

McAdoo came over with his date and they shook hands all the way around. They sat down together.

"Congratulations on graduating Mike. We made it didn't we?" declared McAdoo. "This is Gail. She graduated from Atkinson High, today. We've known each other for about six months."

Gail was a blonde with wavy hair. She came up to McAdoo's eye level. She looked okay.

"Good meeting you, Gail," said Mike, standing up. "My friend here is Jennifer. She graduated with us today."

McAdoo saluted her and said, "How do you do?"

"How's it going with my dad and you at the yard?" asked Mike.

"Really good," said McAdoo. "He's good to me."

"You're still wearing your grad clothes!" exclaimed Mike.

"I haven't been home yet to change," he explained.

"We're getting ready to leave, Randy. We've been here a long time. Let's practice together this summer. I'll be at the rink a lot."

"Sounds good," said McAdoo, standing up.

∽

Jennifer and Mike walked outside and stood looking at the night.

"We didn't finish our pizza," muttered Mike.

Jennifer laughed hard, thinking Mike was a funny guy.

"You want to walk somewhere?" asked Mike.

"Let's go over by the car," she said. "I walk plenty."

Mike took her left hand in his and they went over to the pickup truck.

Wisner was sitting in Mary Jane's living room. She and Herb had gone out to the Boston Market to try out their food. It turned out to be so-so. Oh well, they thought, "You live and learn".

Her parents, Fred and Carol, were sitting with them. Wisner was slightly hunched over in his chair. Mary Jane sat with her hands folded on her lap.

"You guys have it bad, don't you," remarked her dad.

"Yeah," replied Wisner. "I guess so."

"You're both going to Madison, huh?" commented her dad.

"If she gets her scholarship, yeah," answered Wisner.

"You going to live in the dorms?" asked her mom.

"I think they recommend the freshmen do that," said Wisner.

"Well, that may help keep you apart some," said her mom.

"They're giving me a half-scholarship," interjected Wisner.

"He's a brain, Dad," said Mary Jane, looking down at her hands.

"What's your major going to be?" asked her dad.

"Electronic engineering," replied Wisner.

"You going out for the hockey team?" asked her dad.

"I'm going to try out," said Wisner. "If I don't make it, I'll play club hockey."

"Well, that's a plus," said her dad. "I have a soft spot in my heart for hockey players."

"You played, huh Mr. Evans," inquired Wisner.

"Yeah, but I was a center. You're just a defenseman," he smiled.

Wisner gestured apologetically with open hands.

"You kids better watch out," cautioned her mother.

"I will watch out for sure." promised Wisner, nodding his blond head. "But I do love your daughter. That's for sure. Can we date, this summer?"

❧

Jennifer and Mike leaned back against the door of the pickup. They were still in the Pizza World lot.

"I'm a little concerned about being in the car with you. I don't want us to get carried away," fretted Jennifer.

Mike put his arm around her and pulled her close to him.

"Okay, I'll just hold you close out here," replied Mike. "Take your glasses off, please. They're getting in my way. You don't have to see me."

They both snickered at that.

She put her glasses into her coat pocket then put her arm around his neck. He held her closer and put his hand on the back of her head. They turned their heads toward each other and put their lips together. After a moment, he admitted to her,

"This really could get out of control."

Her body felt good against his.

"Jesus! Is this really happening to me?" he exclaimed.

He tilted his head back a little and said, "You're really good looking."

"You better take me home where my mom can protect me," she told him.

❧

He opened the door and she got in. He got into the driver's seat and backed out, then turned toward the exit and drove out. Five minutes later, he parked in front of her building and jumped out. He came around the backside and opened her door.

"C'mon out, you're home," he announced.

Upstairs, she opened the door with her key and let them in. It was 10:00 PM. She went to the wet bar and got him an Evian water. Her mom looked out of her bedroom door and came out.

"Is that it for tonight?" she asked.

"That's it, Mom," Jennifer answered. "Mike came up to say goodnight."

"Now what?" inquired her mother.

Mike assumed she was talking to him.

"Hi, Betty Ann," he responded, pausing briefly, then continued. "I'm going to work at the rink, practice skating, play some pickup hockey, and I don't know what else. My dad might need me at the yard. Oh, and I'm going to read some books."

"What books?" her mom asked.

Mike sat down on the davenport. "I'm going to check out a law book and read about business law," he said. "Maybe I'll read Trump's book, too."

"You sound very ambitious, Michael," she said, impressed with him.

"Mike and I were getting cozy so we came home early," said Jennifer, wryly.

"Yes, I know cozy," said her mother, in acknowledgement.

Mike looked at Jennifer standing next to a chair. He took a drink from his Evian. Then he took another drink.

"Can I call you this summer?" he asked.

"You can call me," she said. "But not too often."

"What if I don't?" he asked.

"Then I'll be mad," she replied.

"We're talking in front of your mom, you know?" he said.

"I know," she replied.

Mike stood up holding the water bottle and walked over to the bar and sat it down.

"You know it's tough being seventeen," he informed her mother.

"It gets tougher," her mom replied.

"I guess, I'll say goodnight," said Mike.

Jennifer walked him to the door and hugged him.

"Thanks for everything. I love you," she whispered.

Mike walked down the stairs and went out the door. He got into the pickup and headed home.

Chapter 24
Summer of Surprises

Mike had worked the Friday after graduation. He went back to the rink the following Monday to sharpen skates and to drive the Zamboni that morning before the figure skaters took to the ice. He got there at 6:00 AM to fire up the machine. There were a half-dozen girls waiting to practice. Some brought their mothers. He rolled out of the garage, onto the ice, turned around and circled around on the ice. When he finished making ice, he waved the girls in and locked up the Zamboni. He walked around the ice towards the workroom. Ernie had checked out his work and gave him the go-ahead on the sharpening operation. The blades were shorter on the figure skates so they didn't take very long. He only found two pair on the sharpening table. He went to talk it over with Ernie in the main office.

Ernie was just hanging up the phone as Mike walked in.

"I wasn't sure you were in boss," he greeted Ernie. "There are only two pairs of skates on the table to be sharpened."

Ernie looked at him and said, "I've got more. I got side tracked. Have you ever met the owner of this rink?"

Mike shook his head.

"You just met him. I'm the new owner," said Ernie. "That's what I was on the phone about."

"Huh," answered Mike. "That's great."

"The old owner was living out of town, in Connecticut. He had some complicated stuff going on with his financial investments. He decided to unload the rink. I bought it."

"Well, good luck with it," exclaimed Mike, reaching his hand out to Ernie. "I'm glad to hear it. I have a closer relationship with the operation now."

Ernie got up from his desk and went to rental room with Mike. He grabbed a few pair lying on the counter and told Mike to get the rest of them. They took them into the workroom and Mike went to work sharpening them.

"I mostly sharpen them by section without checking the blades. If the blades look okay, don't sharpen them," explained Ernie.

Mike started the grinder and started on one of the skates.

"Hey Skates," Ernie called to him as he was going back to the office. "If you have any suggestions or good advice for me, let me know. Okay?"

"The only thing I can suggest right now is what my dad taught me," answered Mike. "Always be honest."

"I hear ya, Skates. I hear ya!"

᠅

That night Mike had been thinking of ways to build up business at the rink. He came to the conclusion that meant bringing in more skaters. His idea, which he would submit to Ernie was to offer low income skating classes so that more people would learn how to skate which would in turn, increase the number of skaters frequenting the rink. He would offer to do the teaching. Another idea was to give customers a "Happy Hour" in which admission would be cheaper. A ladies night would help out. He decided he would write these ideas down in the morning.

Ice Rink

❦

Monday nights were usually open for pickup games at the rink. Mike, Hurstmeyer, and McAdoo were there to mix it up. Some of the others were guys on college teams and some thirtyish guys there reliving their playing days. This night there were only ten skaters there.

"Okay you guys, remember the rules. No checking and no slap shots. We don't have any goalies." The speaker was one of the older guys, named Danny.

They chose up teams and Mike and McAdoo were on the same team. The guys were wearing old practice uniforms so one team wore yellow swatches pinned to their shirts to better identify them. Some of the guys had holes in their jerseys and long stockings. There were no referees there so they just tossed the puck up into the air at center ice and took off from there. They tried not to go offside during the game. It was good practice for the recent graduates, playing with experienced men. The puck handling was very intricate or so it seemed. Mike and his pals learned a lot about passing. The guys playing defense showed off a lot of their stick work. Mike was glad there was no checking. He didn't want to try and bump these guys. McAdoo was having a hard time getting by these guys. After about a half-hour, they took a break.

Mike found out one of the college guys played for River Falls. He told Mike to go out for the team. Some of the older guys were talking about the Blackhawks and the pro teams. Hurstmeyer told Mike he was going to one of the smaller private schools that had a hockey team. McAdoo said he was going to a community college and would play club hockey.

After the break, they took to the ice to practice some more. Before they got started, Mike noticed a dark haired guy walking outside the closed in ice surface looking around. The guy looked to be in his mid twenties. He had never seen the guy before. Most of the other onlookers, he recognized as regulars. For some reason, Mike had a uneasy feeling about the stranger. There was no public skating on Monday nights but the doors were open to visitors. They played hard, with the puck changing hands a lot and the skaters working up a big sweat. When they called a halt, the participants high-fived each other and went to the dressing room. Mike looked around the rink for the dark haired guy but he didn't see him around.

※

Ernie put Mike to work on Thursday nights as well as Fridays. Mike had given Ernie his ideas about "Happy Hour" and skating lessons to build up patronage. Ernie thanked him for the good advice. Mike was behind the rental counter on a Thursday night in July. He had been there in the late afternoon, sharpening skates. As it turned out, the summer heat had prompted the local skaters to frequent the rink more. The admission receipts were building up. Kids from the high school were coming up to the counter saying, "Hi", to him. Ernie had put up a sign next to the counter to advertise 1/2 price "Happy Hour" on Wednesdays at 4:00 PM till 8:00 PM. About 9:00 that night, he saw the same dark haired stranger walk by the counter. He had no bag or skates with him. Mike watched him. He didn't stay long. After walking around the rink once, he left. Mike was still wary of him. He didn't fit in, somehow.

※

At 5:00 PM, there was scattering of joggers circling the track at the high school. Two of them were Wisner and Mary Jane utilizing their time together for the right reasons. They were wearing their shorts and tee shirts. Wisner was huffing and puffing along trying to keep up with his girl friend, the track star.

"Slow down, Janie! You're not racing," he beseeched her. "I don't want you to get away from me and wind up with some other guy!"

"No other guy can keep up with me," she laughed, slowing down.

"We're just jogging," he reminded her.

"How far do you want to go?" she asked.

"Two or three miles," he responded. "I'm not in that good of shape yet."

"What do you hear from U of W?" he asked her, after a time.

"They said okay when they saw my racing record," she replied. "I forgot to tell you."

"So you've got a full scholarship?" he pressed on.

"Yeah, all the way, year by year," she replied.

"Good!" he exclaimed. "I'm glad I took a chance and enrolled with them."

After forty minutes or so, they stopped and walked over to the chain link fence. Wisner leaned down with his hands on his knees. His triceps were clearly defined in that position. He looked up at her sweaty face under her headband and laughed.

"I see you in the least attractive circumstances and I still love you."

"We're going to have to love each other, carefully," she cautioned.

He gazed at her hazel eyes, straight nose, and well formed lips and felt lucky. Her body was beautiful and for that he felt even luckier.

⚜

The Friday night crowd came into the rink as Mike was finishing his Zamboni run. Ernie was manning the rental counter while Mike put the ice surfacing machine into its holding room. They needed another helper to keep the rink running smoother. Mike was aware of this deficiency but he kept it to himself. It wasn't his place to tell Ernie how to run the rink operation. Ernie had to keep his expenses down.

He took over the rental counter and Ernie left to make his rounds to make sure things were in good shape. He had to check the thermostat on the freezing apparatus. A lot of the high school kids were coming back to skate with no schoolwork to worry about. Rental counts were running high this night. About 7:30, the rentals were slowing down a bit. Mike looked over the activity on the ice. He wondered if the younger kids out skating would evolve into hockey players. The ones wearing hockey skates were the one's most likely to take up the sport. At about 7:45, Mike saw the dark haired stranger walk by carrying a bag. He watched him closely as he headed for the benches. A moment later, he went on by still carrying his bag. He hadn't changed into skates. This made Mike very nervous. He picked up the phone and called 911. The voice answering asked what the problem was. Mike spoke tersely into the phone.

"There's a dangerous looking person inside the Laketown ice rink. I think he might be here to do somebody harm. You better hurry."

Mike pressed the hang up button and called Ernie's number. No answer. He grabbed the "Back in Five minutes" sign and put it on the counter. He hid the money drawer in a skate shelf and shot out the door into the rink area. He headed to where the stranger had gone.

He thought to himself, "This may be a false alarm but I'm not going to take any chances." The news was rife with stories of terrorist attacks on large groups of people. He saw the stranger in one corner of the building doing something on the floor. He ran back to the office and grabbed a flashlight, then came back out. He shined the light at the stranger working on the floor. The man stopped and looked up.

"What are you doing there, buddy?" he called out.

There was no answer. Just then Ernie came trotting up.

"What's going on?" he asked.

"There's a guy doing something over there on the floor!" he exclaimed, pointing the flashlight in that direction.

"I'm going back for my gun!" shouted Ernie.

Just then two men in uniform rushed in the front door and looked around.

"Over here!" yelled Ernie. "There's a guy in here acting strange."

One of the cops scanned the area with his strong flashlight and illuminated the suspect, crouching on the floor. He had his bag open and was putting something together.

"Stay where you are mister!" called out one of the cops. "Lie face down on the floor and don't move!"

The suspect didn't lie down. Instead, he made a move to get out of the light.

"Lie face down on the floor or we'll shoot!" warned the cop.

The stranger lay down on the floor.

"Stay here guys!" ordered one of the cops as they went to check out the stranger.

The cop cuffed the guy from behind and pulled him upright. The other cop picked up something on the floor and put it into the bag. He inspected the area with his light then picked up the bag. The cops came back to Ernie and Mike prodding the stranger in front of them.

They stopped and one pointed his beam at the stranger's face. The man grimaced in the light.

"Do you know this guy?" one of them asked.

"Not me," replied Ernie.

"I've noticed him hanging out here for a couple of days," said Mike. "Never saw him before that. I never saw him go out on the ice."

"What's in the bag?" asked Ernie.

"Oh he was just putting together a rifle. That's all," replied the officer.

Mike looked around and noticed a dozen or so skaters standing behind them. One of the officers had his report pad out filling out a report. After a minute, he handed it to Ernie to see.

"Sign at the bottom," instructed the officer.

Ernie signed it and handed the pad back. At that the cops left leading the suspect out the door and back to the police car.

Ernie looked down at the gun he was holding, a 32-caliber revolver. He looked at Mike and said to the skaters,

"Okay folks. You can go back and skate now."

He told Mike to go back to the rental room and he went back to his office holding his gun. There were groups of skaters and spectators milling around, talking about the incident.

∾

After closing time, Mike went into Ernie's office and returned the flashlight he had taken. He laid the money drawer down on the desk. Ernie leaned back in his chair and looked at him.

"How'd you know where the flashlight was?" he inquired.

"It was sitting on your desk," explained Mike.

"Who called the cops?" asked Ernie.

"I did, of course," replied Mike.

"You knew he had a rifle?" asked Ernie.

"Not really," said Mike, still breathing hard. "The guy looked suspicious to me. He was walking around with this bag."

Ernie looked down at the gun on his desk and just sat there.

"Goodnight, Skates," he said. "See you on your next shift."

※

On the next Tuesday morning, Mike and Wisner were skating up and down the ice with their hockey sticks, passing the puck back and forth. The figure skaters had finished their time on the ice an hour earlier and public skating wouldn't start until 6:30 that night. They skated forward to one end and then backwards to the other end.

"The word's out that you had some excitement here last Friday night," commented Wisner.

"It was damned exciting," replied Mike. "Some weirdo brought a disassembled rifle into the place in a bag and was getting ready to use it. We stopped him just in time."

"Thank God for that," said Wisner.

"Yeah, the cops took him away," said Mike.

※

The two friends were leaning up against the boards talking about the fall semester.

"So you and Evans got scholarships to Madison, huh?" asked Mike.

"Yeah, we're an item now," said Wisner. "We've gotta watch it. She's gonna run track!"

"Well, I'm going to River Falls, you know. Yeah, I already told you."

"Anything doing with Jennifer?" asked Wisner.

"No, she wants to play it safe," replied Mike. "She may be going to Madison, too. She's working at the hospital this summer. I guess I'm floating around adrift for a while."

※

A girl walked into the rink holding a pair of silver figure skates by the laces. She walked around to where the boys were talking. They watched silently as she approached.

"Hi, Evelyn," both of the boys said in unison.

"Hi to you, too, she countered.

"How'd you get in?" asked Mike. "The rink's closed."

"Well, I called the office here and said I wanted Mike Thomas to teach me how to skate," she explained. "They told me you were here today and to come right down."

Wisner was looking down at his stick moving the puck around, with one hand.

Mike looked at her quietly. She had on some kind of khaki pants and a long sleeved white shirt. She looked great, as usual. Her blond hair was kind of shoulder length.

"Are you okay to skate with me?" inquired Mike. "Your boyfriend warned me to keep my distance."

"No, it's okay," she answered.

"Well, what about your boyfriend, Johnny Football?" he asked, tilting his head.

"We broke up," she replied.

"What about him? Did he break up too?" asked Mike.

Wisner picked up the puck and announced, "I gotta go, Mike. We'll talk later."

"Let me know if you wanta play pickup, okay?" Mike called to him.

Wisner got off the ice and went to take off his skates.

∽

"Look, I'll skate with you but I don't want to tangle with your boyfriend." explained Mike. "What kind of skating do I teach you? I don't figure skate."

"Just skate with me, that's all," she said, looking at him strangely.

"Why'd you break up with Heller?" asked Mike, still doubtful.

"Let's go over to the benches," she suggested. "I want to put on my skates."

∽

They went to the benches and sat down. She took off her step-in shoes.

"He's not my kind of guy," she said. "He wants to get married and have babies right away. He wants to go to college, play football, and maybe coach or get into retail afterwards. I want to go to college, too and go to law school before I get saddled with a family."

"So you want to study law, too," commented Mike.

"Yeah and maybe go to work for Fox News later," she added.

"My parents watch Fox News," said Mike.

She laced up her skates and stood up.

"One big question, why me?" he asked.

"You're my kind of guy," she replied. "You're a high achiever. And I like you too, more than you know."

"You like me?" asked Mike, in disbelief.

"Yes, I like you," she answered.

"I guess I like you too," said Mike. "But you know that we're both kids. We're not even eighteen yet."

"Thanks for reminded me, Mike," she acknowledged.

"Come on out on the ice and I'll watch you," he offered.

They glided out on the ice and faced each other.

"One more thing," he injected, after a moment of thought. "You're so damned good looking, it's hard for me to believe all this is happening."

⁕

Jennifer Lundberg was sitting alone at a table in the hospital lunchroom. She was reading a medical magazine as she ate her salad. She had on an orange hospital jumpsuit. A young orderly in a similar orange jumpsuit sat down across from her and asked,

"Do you mind if I sit here?"

She looked at him and said, "It's alright, go ahead, but I'm not getting involved in any relationship I want you to know."

The guy laughed and said, "You're new here aren't you?"

"Yes," she answered. "I just graduated from high school. I'm not eighteen yet. I'm going to the university in the fall and I'm going to graduate."

"I hear you," responded the guy. "I just liked your looks."

She stared at him for a moment and said, "Well, it's okay. You can sit here."

Made in the USA
Monee, IL
26 February 2025